The *Saga* of
Diversion *Lily*

FEATURING
DOMESTIC LILAC

Diversion Lily

Fulton Books
Meadville, PA

Published by Fulton Books 2023

ISBN 978-1-64952-783-7 (paperback)
ISBN 978-1-64952-784-4 (digital)

Printed in the United States of America

ACKNOWLEDGMENTS

I APPRECIATE GOD FOR BESTOWING upon me the capacity to catch creative ideas and express them in writing. My intentions are to empower individuals who have been victims of domestic abuse or sexual assault, and I hope you find strength in my tale.

Special thanks to my niece @jilikejass for pouring her heart and soul into the book cover. With every brush, you caught my beauty and anguish. I adore you. I want to include a special thank-you to @pickaplate and @birdskitchendc for allowing me to showcase your business. Your food is so delicious! I wish you much success! Shout out to my sister, you rock and rule!

Thank you to every one of my friends and family who supported me in finishing the narrative. You are aware of who you are.

I want to thank everyone who helped me finish *The Saga of Diversion Lily featuring Domestic Lilac* whether directly or indirectly.

Also, without further ado, a big thank-you to everyone who helped make this narrative a reality. Because some of the events in this book are true to reality, your identities have been altered to protect the innocent. You made it happen. Please accept my apologies if I failed to name anybody along the way; I blame it on my brain, not my heart.

Get up when you're shoved down in the mud and create mud pies! After that, tidy up. Unless you want it to, no domestic relationship stays the same! The term *violence* is not associated with the household in the dictionary. That, too, can change.

It is incredibly difficult to realign your life and regain your innocence after any domestic offense. My heart goes out to everyone who has been harmed by domestic violence (physical, sexual, or emotional abuse). The most frequent kind of violence against women and children is domestic and sexual violence. It affects women throughout their lives.

From sex-selective abortions on female fetuses to forced suicide and mental torture, abuse in all formations is seen to some extent in every community on the planet. It is not an option to remain silent anymore. If you are experiencing physical, sexual, emotional, or physical abuse, please contact your local hotlines and share your information.

You can recover from trauma!

I hope you enjoy reading!

Dig deep and stay strong.

domestic [duh-mes-tik]

adjective
of or relating to the home, the household, household affairs,
or the family: domestic pleasures; devoted to home life
or household affairs; no longer wild; tame; domesticated:
domestic animals; of or relating to one's own or a particular
country as apart from other countries: domestic trade.

noun
a hired household servant.
something produced or manufactured in one's own country

INTRODUCTION

Behind the veil...

IT WAS THE STROKE OF midnight when the doorway to the bedroom crept open. He turned the doorknob and entered cautiously. The moonlight prematurely invited him inside the densely dark room. A thick frame of a man stood inside the frame of the doorway. His hands were empty. His pulse and heartbeat racing as he stared at the angelic body on the bed. His mind capturing mental lustful images. The fire inside his loins grew as he began to stroke his manhood. His eyes set on his target. He'd decided that tonight was the perfect opportunity to make his move. Her innocence be demanded. This moment would forever be their secret. The cost of her silence was not an issue. He was willing to do anything to have his way. As his blood continued to boil over, he watched her closely as she tossed and turned inside the ruffled sheets. Her soft dewy skin dripped with purity and sensual essence of an un-blossomed flower. Occasionally, a soft moan would escape her baby lips as she dreamed of sunflowers and unicorns on her pillow. Her hair could not be tamed as it spread across her pillow. Her barely black tresses caressed her soft round shoulders during the day as she ran through the endless violets. Her laugh was magnetic as she giggled and raced without fear and no worry crowding her mind. She was just a girl violet eyes and sweet as the honeydew. Her round face and curiosity enraptured his membrane and made her desirable in an unfamiliar way. She looked at him with love and curiosity in her beautiful violet eyes. She clung to his hand on the first day she walked inside the mansion. Afraid of what hidden thing would cause her heart to patter rapidly, she found him standing in the hallway willing to comfort her anxiety.

In his mind, it was fate and opportunity that had brought them together on this full moon night. He wanted someone fresh and beautiful to share his horrid dark desires with at night. A soul to cool the intense fire in his loins.

، Her name was Lilac. She was perfect and his for the taking.

The porcelain walls and sparkling diamond chandelier of the mansion were void of noise. Not a soul stirred the rooms or disrupted the sleep of the rich and wealthy. Every eye rested peacefully unto a fluffy pillow. His name was Sammy. The oldest male child of the Chad family. Sammy had waited for the right time to cross the empty hallway of Lilac's room. He watched her from his hidden camera inside his room as Lilac and her little sister, Daisy, recited their prayers and crawled into bed, her favorite soft pink nightgown adorning her milky light skin. Sammy waited patiently as his parents wandered off to bed. First, his aging mother, Jade, with her luke-warm wine and then Jack, his father, with stress lines dancing across his face. Sammy wanted Lilac all to himself.

As he stood silently inside Lilac's doorway, he realized he needed to be quick and sweet. He'd worked out all the details inside his head after fondling himself. He did not want Lilac to scream; that would ruin everything. Sammy was not a newcomer. He had robbed many young women of their essence. Some at different ages in their journey. Each one was not considered to be a victim in Sammy's mind. In his eyes, he was giving them the love and companionship that they would eventually desire from a man of his caliber. Their silence could be bought, and no one would ever believe their word over his.

Lilac pushed the duvet cover with her painted pink toenails and glitter polish on her tiny fingers. She was sleeping peacefully in her queen size, extra fluffy bed when she felt a hand touch her face. Her eyes fluttered open as she skipped a breath. She could not see his face. His masculine silhouette stood in the reflection of the window. His cold hands trembled across Lilac's face. Her breath trapped inside her throat. Lilac's heart began to race as she searched for a scream inside the oversized dark room. She was scared, alone, and afraid of what would happen. Her mother was too far away to run to her side. Lilac bucked her eyes wide and tried to recognize the face and body of the person standing in front of her. Her eyes blinked rapidly as her brain tried to catch up.

Sammy placed his index finger over her mouth with his free hand. Tears began to well inside Lilac's eyes. She searched around the room for an exit. The door was closed. She didn't know if he had locked it. Her room rested on the corner of the mansion, two floors above ground level. A balcony that overlooked the roaming lawn of endless grass and beautiful flowers. Lilac had a view most would die for, but in this moment, she was trapped with a sexual predator. Lilac began to tremble in fear. Her eyes began to moisten as she squinted her eyes to see in the darkness. He looked vaguely familiar; Lilac began to suspect.

His words were void inside his room. Sammy slowly began to climb into the bed. His hand never left Lilac's mouth. His lean muscular physique towered over her fragile frame. The tears from Lilac's eyes began to fall onto Sammy's hand. Her tears didn't disturb his desire and curiosity to explore her body. He wanted to sample the warmth of her innocence and devour her with his member. Sammy began to push Lilac further onto the bed. The bed squeaked with each motion. Sammy came into clear focus as Lilac could see his face more clearly in the moonlight. She could hardly believe her eyes. Sammy was more than a cousin; he was like a big brother. Lilac tried her best to wrap her ten-year-old mind around the reason for the visit in the middle of the night.

"Sammy…," Lilac mumbled through her tears.

Her cries fell on deaf ears as Sammy pierced her tears with an evil glare in his eyes. His warm and happy spirit had left his body. He was cold and void of emotion and rational thought.

"Be quiet," Sammy demanded.

Lilac began to wipe her salty tears as she clenched the covers underneath. She pulled on the sheets with all her strength. Sammy rested his body in front of Lilac on the bed. Her legs were trapped underneath the weight of his frame. Slowly Sammy began to push Lilac back onto the pillow. Briefly lifting his body from the bed,

Sammy pushes the cover away from the bed. Her vulnerable ten-year-old body was exposed in the darkness of light. Lilac wanted to scream as tears began to flow down her plump cheeks. She stared terrified into Sammy's mahogany brown eyes. He licked his thin pink lips and grazed Lilac cheek with his right hand. Lilac began to tremble at his touch.

"What are you going to do to me?" Lilac mumbled.

With a blink of an eye, Sammy raised his hand and covered Lilac's mouth. He stared into her watery, round violet eyes. His cold blood and reckless thoughts compounding him to keep going until his ripe flesh was satisfied.

Sammy whispered. "I want you to lay back on the bed and do as ask," Sammy instructed.

"Are you going to hurt me?"

Sammy grinned. He knew his mature thoughts would traumatize Lilac for life. That wasn't his plan. He desired to have her within reach and ready to quench his obsessively sadistic sexual urges. Women his age could never satisfy the depth of fire inside his groins.

Lilac obliges Sammy's orders as she slowly rests her back against the cold pillow. Lilac begins to squeeze her violet-hued eyes tight to stop the tears from running down her cheek. She glances at the closed bedroom door in the distance. Thoughts of running and screaming for help enter her thoughts. Anxiously predicting that someone will save her from the bad monster in his bed. Sammy glances over his shoulder mockingly. He knows that Lilac could try to run for help. But his girth and long arms would conquer Lilac within a matter of seconds. Her defenseless ten-year-old body would be no match for his 170-pound body. Breaking a sweat to tame Lilac would be too much work. Sammy was pleased so far that Lilac had not caused too much trouble. Unlike the others, she was a good girl.

Sammy began to run his hand up and down Lilac bare legs. As his hand reached the pinnacle of her womanhood, Lilac began to plead for Sammy to stop and not go any further. Sammy had had enough of her tears and squeezed her neck with his unoccupied hand. He could feel the blood pulsating through Lilac's neck as she struggled to breathe. Lilac began to scratch Sammy's arm as she fought for her next breath. The sheets on the bed began to ruffle as Sammy climbed on top of Lilac. The once pristine bed fit for a man was now the scene of a trauma. Sammy jumped on top of Lilac and whispered inside her ear.

"Stop screaming," he warned. "Close your eyes and I'll go away. I promise."

Lilac couldn't believe a word that Sammy whispered in her ear. Her heart climbed inside her throat. She was terrified of Sammy. Her desire to live became more important than her fears. Lilac closed her eyes and pretended she was somewhere far off into a land of make believe. Lilac's body felt numb as Sammy began to plant lukewarm kisses all over her face and chest. His moans played rapidly inside her ear as he robbed Lilac of her innocence in the night. Lilac closed her eyes and wondered if God was watching. If He was watching, why couldn't he save her from the monster? It was on this night that Lilac realized everything that she once knew was a lie, and that if she was going to survive, she would have to become a monster too.

CHAPTER 1

Blind Shoots

THE LIGHT FROM THE BROKEN window inside the crack house stirred her awake. Jacky opened her swollen eyes. Her eyes began to adjust to her surroundings quickly. The smell of piss and shit simmered across her nose. Jacky wasn't alone. Two bodies rested unevenly across the small bedroom floor. One male. One female. Both over the age of twenty-one. Jacky began to stumble her way into dabbing her bruised cheek. Her matted hair and rotten moist clothes clung to the dankness in her once light skin. Broken glass rested underneath her exposed feet. Jacky began to crawl around the broken glass on the floor that rested near the mattress on the floor of the bathroom. She'd gone to the crack house to score. With only the clothes on her back and a few dollars in her pocket, Jacky was searching for freedom inside a drug. Getting high on a regular basis had become her new normal. Jacky was far from her humble beginnings.

Once, Jacky became too troublesome for her family. Getting pregnant at an early age was not a part of her family's plan for her life. Jacky did not want to follow her mother's footsteps. She wanted more than having a house filled with kids and a decent husband. Jacky desired a life of glitz and glamour. She never wanted to just settle for what life could give her. Jacky was a rebel with a fiery heart. Her mother, Jade, feared that Jacky would negatively influence her

1

siblings, Theodore, Sammy, and Ava. She knew that out of her four children, Jacky would be the one to ruin the family legacy. Her wild and reckless behavior was ruining the family reputation. Everywhere they went, people would talk about Jacky being a problem and how they didn't want her around. Relationships were being threatened. Business deals were stalled. All because of Jacky.

Jade realized Jacky had to go. She was too much of a problem for the family. Determined to do the right thing Jade opted to sway Jacky to leave the home immediately with a promise to give Jacky a $50,000 deposit into her private account. Jade knew Jacky could never refuse the money. Jade and her family were a part of an influential family in the hills of California. Jade and her husband had built a successful empire by offering custom furniture. With over forty years of success in business, Jade and her husband had made a household name for her family. With money comes power and influence, and Jade understood that better than Jacky. When her teenage daughter became pregnant, it was a disgrace unto the entire family. People began to mock the family name and judge Jade for her parenting skills. Jade loved her daughter Jacky dearly. But she soon realized that Jacky was too much of a risk and would have to be dealt with in some way.

Jade was not willing to allow Jacky to destroy the family name. She knew people would talk for years to come. But she knew also that if a problem arose in her family, she had to get rid of it quickly and quietly.

Jade made up her mind that Jacky was an utter embarrassment to the family empire. There was nothing Jade could do with Jacky any longer. There was nothing money couldn't solve. Jade made up her mind that the family would be better off without Jacky. That if she was around, she would be toxic and deadly to the entire family. Jade realized Jacky needed tough love. Jacky would be able to provide for herself as a young woman. The only condition to accepting the money would be that Jacky would have to leave town forever and never return to the family home. Jacky refused to accept the money. She didn't want to be bought out of her own family.

Jade confided in her husband, Jack, that she was in a lot of pain. Jack could not bear his wife's suffering. He promised Jacky a new life if she decided to start over fresh somewhere else. Jacky knew she would resent her parents for the rest of her life. But she figured the money could be used to help take care of her. With resentment in her heart, Jacky accepted her parents' offer and moved across the country. Jacky took the fifty thousand dollars and relocated to Northeast corridor of Washington DC.

She didn't know much about DC. However, Jacky was a quick study; it took no time to figure out the town. Growing up in California had made Jacky familiar with gang bangers, hustlers, and rich old men. She was equipped with her street PhD.

She chose to relocate to in Ward 5 quadrium better known as "Trinidad" in Northeast Washington DC. A four-bedroom, two-story home Jack bought before moving to California. It was an enormous change from the mansion, scenic views, and the nightlife in California.

When Jacky packed her belongings and left in the middle of the night, she vowed to never see her family again. If they didn't want her at her worst, they didn't deserve her at her best.

Unknown to Jade, her daughter did not arrive in DC alone. She brought her chaperone Stephen. Steven helped Jacky to settle into her new life comfortably. Stephen wasn't just Jacky's chaperone. He was also the father of her baby girl, Lilac, who was due in a few months.

During the first few months of living in DC, Jacky found her drug connection to flip the money by purchasing marijuana and powder cocaine. She had Stephen's help transporting drugs from California to DC. She quickly became the "star" in her newfound neighborhood, selling marijuana by the pound and powdered cocaine by the gram.

Jacky became familiar with the culture, adapting to Go-Go music Rare Essence, Experience Unlimited, Chuck Brown, and Little Benny and the Masters. By the time she gave birth to Lilac, she was a local celebrity.

A safe full of money and clientele of a madame, Jacky felt indispensable. With Stephen as a "mule," Jacky figured the only tool she needs to survive in this game is her baby daddy. Stephen was there to support Jacky's every need if rocking with the life of fast money.

In between Stephen traveling from California to DC, selling drugs and making lots of money, Jacky became pregnant with her second child, Daisy.

Jacky began to think that the drug life was not what she wanted to present to Lilac and Daisy. She renewed her lifestyle, while pregnant with Daisy. She took a few sewing classes and began to slow down. Before you know it, Jacky stopped selling drugs and became a seamstress serving the elite in Georgetown, Bethesda, and Chevy Chase, Maryland.

Stephen saw the changes in Jacky, and never uttered a word of how he felt about her new lifestyle. Stephen got dressed and told Jacky he was going to Wings & More and More Wings on the corner of H Street Northeast. That was the last time Jacky laid eyes on Stephen, leaving Jacky with two beautiful girls to raise alone.

Having two children forced Jacky to become a better person. She no longer had time to play in the streets. Jacky was looking to change her life for the betterment of her two flowers she adorns. They were all that really mattered.

Years went by as Jacky learned to mend her broken heart. The more time went by, Jacky had learned to live without Stephen and her family being in her life, she could not ignore the signs that she is now a few years older, had soon realized that life had dealt her a bad hand, but she was strong enough to handle any curve balls.

Jacky often dreamed of a life without her children. She desired to go back in time and make some changes. Starting with becoming a mother too soon. Jacky's desires to be a household name for designing clothes for some of the world's most beautiful women in DC clouded her mind daily. Jacky began to accept she made a lot of mistakes and wasn't ready for adulthood. Jacky often thought of the years of her being a teenage mother and how her fast lifestyle destroyed her future.

Jacky often thought of how she made the best life possible for Lilac and Daisy under the circumstances of having two children before she was twenty years old. She felt she gave Daisy and Lilac the best of both worlds' sweetness and truth. It was all she really had, after giving up on the life of fast money. It was Jacky's real definition of what she considered as "rich" and love.

As Lilac grew older, Jacky could understand something clearly, at last, looking inside her once-blossoming daughters eyes dim, although Lilac could express herself clearly. Jacky slightly converted back into her old habits of selling drugs and could see that she was doing more harm than good in her daughter's life. Lilac watched closely as her mom sold drugs to her friends' parents. The kids often teased Lilac and Daisy about their mother, calling her the Queen of the Crack. They were often getting into fights defending Jacky. Jacky soon realized that she would have to make the toughest decision of her life.

CHAPTER 2

Peace Lily

ONCE THE MONEY DRIED UP and being watched by the police constantly, Jacky knew it was time to make a move to California. There was nothing left in Washington, DC for Jacky. Everywhere she looked, all she could see was heartache and pain. Every night, Jacky would look into the broken and distraught faces of her girls for answers. The answers would never come overnight. Jacky knew that her girls deserved stability and security. That was something she couldn't provide into their lives. No matter how much she loved Lilac and Daisy. Jacky had to admit she needed help.

Jacky knew she could never go back to her family home. Jacky was too prideful to beg anyone for a second chance. She'd spiraled into the abyss of darkness chasing her promising dreams of stardom in the hills of California during her teenage years. Her dreams had allowed her naiveté to go unchecked. With her barely black skin, fine long black hair, womanly hips, and round violet eyes that could hypnotize any man, Jacky knew she could make it in Hollywood or anywhere in the world. It was just a matter of time before she was discovered. But in hindsight, Jacky realized early on in life that the life she wanted would mean sacrificing her children. Jacky loved her children, Lilac and Daisy. She loved them more than anything in this world. But Jacky knew she wasn't quite ready. Her life was just beginning, and her dreams were more real than she could ever imagine. But none of that would be possible with two babies on each hip. Jacky had to make a choice—a choice that mothers across the world make daily—to sacrifice their motherhood for dreams or choose motherhood and sacrifice your dreams. Jacky chose her dreams. She figured that her chance at making it big in California would pay off sooner than later. She knew that she would be able to give her girls the life they deserved someday. But everything rested on her decisions today. There were days that Jacky could not feed or clothe Lilac and Daisy. Some days, she had to go without eating to support them. The bad days definitely outweigh the good. As a single mom, Jacky watched as other women her age was burdened with raising their children alone. Their dreams seemed too far-fetched to ever be reality. Jacky didn't want to end up like those women she saw daily. Every day, Jacky could see her dreams slipping out of her hands. She knew that her parents could give Lilac and Daisy a better upbringing than she could. Being a teenage mom and another statistic was not a part of the plan. Jacky was willing to give up everything to live out her dreams.

It was hard listening to her daughters' cries as they yearned desperately for their mother's love and attention. But Jacky had turned that part of her off permanently. If she was going to make it in the world, she needed to cut the emotional cords.

In the morning, Jacky decided her life would change for the better. She dressed Lilac in her favorite purple tutu and lavender hair bow. Daisy cradled her favorite doll inside her pudgy hands as she danced in her tiara and frilly pink dress. With their bellies filled to the brim with fruit and oats, Jacky kissed her daughters lovingly on the cheek. She stared into her children's big beautiful round eyes and promised them a new adventure. At the time, Lilac was only ten years old. Her inquisitive nature made her special in Jacky's eyes. She always had more questions than Jacky had answers. It hurt Jacky the most when she had to lie to protect her children. Sometimes she had to lie to protect them for her. Jacky couldn't bear the fact that she was about to break her children's hearts forever and there was nothing she could do about it.

Two nights before, Jacky slept in between Lilac and Daisy. She watched them sleep peacefully inside her arms, a daughter on each side. Tears began to well in her eyes within the shadows of the night. Jacky stared at her girls with love in her heart. She prayed silently as she asked God to forgive her for her mistakes. She prayed that someday her girls would love her as much as they do within that moment. Jacky hated herself for having to choose between her girls or her dreams. She knew that someday they would look back and appreciate all the sacrifices and tough choices she made. Jacky couldn't wait for that day to arrive.

Jacky realized that life could only get better from that day forward.

CHAPTER 3

Daffodils

LILAC AND DAISY LOVED EVERYTHING about their mother, the sweetness, bitterness, and the sincerity in her voice. It commanded their attention. Although, deep underneath all the beauty they all hold, they simply hated the truth on specific characteristics about their mother, Jacky. She was full of lies, betrayal, and secrecy.

Lilac and Daisy did not know their extended family members such as their grandparents, aunts, and uncles. Jade and Jack could not imagine what Jacky put them through. There were so many moving components of Jacky. Lilac and Daisy never stood a chance.

It was too much for a ten- and nine-year-old to track. The two youngsters would make jokes during pillow talk at night of how Jackie could've won an Oscar in the category of "Mastering the Art of Deception." She was particularly good at that, and they often wondered how she could have missed her calling as an actress.

"Lilac and Daisy, it's time for supper come wash your hands and face," Jacky yelled out of the window from the four-story home.

Lilac and Daisy stopped laughing and started running up the six flights of steps in rhythm, dashing to see who can sit the fastest and get the best seat at the dinner table. Like a game of musical chairs every evening.

"Oh no, you do not," Jacky said firmly. "No eating at my table with dirty hands. Get up both of you and march your frail behinds to the bathroom!"

"Okay, Jacky!" The girls replied, still giggling and testing who's going to get to the bathroom first to wash their face and hands.

"I taught you better than that, and you must take your manners with you wherever you go," Jacky replied.

"Yes, ma'am," they replied, making funny faces staring at each other in the bathroom.

Lilac and Daisy began to eat as if they hadn't eaten all day. They were signifying with their eyes, while eating, intentions of going back outside to end the night with their friends before the streetlights come on.

"Slow down eating before you choke yourselves," said Jacky with this puzzling look upon her face. Lilac could tell something was on her mind and was wondering what stunt Jacky was up to now.

"I haven't got to the table," Jacky yelled. "I have something to discuss with you two. Lilac, especially you! The need to depend on each other is more crucial than ever. Your sister and your lives depend on it."

"Jacky, am only ten years old. What could I possibly do to save our lives? Oh my, what script you wrote for us now, Jacky? What do you mean 'your lives'?"

"Lilac, mind yourself. I am your mother and not the other way around!"

Lilac thought to herself, *Now you want to act like a mother.* Lilac knew when to yield way of her mouth and thoughts to Jacky.

Before, I would be rudely interrupted by my mother, "Little Miss Lilac."

"Well...there is no uncomplicated way of saying this," Jacky sighed. "I am sending you to live with my sister Jade and her husband, Jack—"

Jack could not complete the sentence, Lilac interjected loudly!

"Jacky, we don't know your sister or her family!" Lilac screamed. Lilac was always quick to respond; she was like Jacky in that sense.

In the same instance, Lilac began to think of their father, Stephen, who took on the role of an absentee father. As if someone paid him to do it.

"Jacky, why? We don't want to go with your family. We don't know them! Are you crazy?" said the ten-year-old Lilac.

"Where is our father? Where is he?" said Lilac. "Jacky, the people that should be present are nowhere around. That's why no one likes you, Jacky. You always tell us lies."

Pop! "Jacky, please don't hit me again! I'm sorry!"

"You are really getting besides yourself little girl. You will learn one day to slow to anger and listen before responding. Stay in a child's lane, little girl!"

Little Daisy didn't utter a word.

"To answer your question, Lilac, concerning your father. Where is Stephen, Lilac? What has he done for you, girly? You tell me since you have all the answers, young lady," said Jacky.

"You probably ran him away," said Lilac. "Jacky, what could have possibly gone so wrong between you and Stephen?" the ten-year-old asked.

"Whatever it was, he never looked for us!"

"You're one mean Momma," said Lilac. "I have to grow up fast. Daisy, come on get up from the table. This lady is putting on a good show today! Give her a round of applause," said the ten-year-old.

Daisy was crying and very confused about why Jacky didn't want them anymore. Daisy would not speak. It was too overwhelming for the nine-year-old little girl to take in. Jacky wasn't playing with a full deck, but they loved her.

"Come on, Daisy. Let's go!" They slowly walk to the room, overcome with grief and sadness.

"Jacky pulled a trick on us this time!" said Daisy.

"Do not come in our room!" Lilac screamed and slammed the door. She found an old piece of blank paper in her book bag. Holding a red crayon, she wrote, "Do Not Enter." Lilac taped the sign on the outside of the bedroom door, plain as day for Jacky to read.

Lilac started talking to Daisy about how Jacky would always joke about how fast her labor was for Lilac! Mimicking their mother's voice, "Lilac came into the world swinging and kicking as if she was running or fighting for her life. Jacky would laugh and joke around in the happiest times."

"Lilac, what is wrong with our mother?"

"Jacky never seems to have it all together. Why play with our minds like that? She's nuts, Daisy. She does not know how to be a mother or a friend! Let us pray that this is a joke, Daisy."

They were shutting completely down from their usual horseplay with friends. Lilac bought comfort to her younger sister by telling her they will live a better life in California.

Lilac began to school Daisy to keep her silence of being black in California. Lilac reminded Daisy of the television series on the assassination of Martin Luther King. It was Jacky's way of reminding herself they were two generations away from revealing their pure bloodline to the world.

*****

"Daisy, it has been three days since we had that dreadful conversation at the dinner table. Daisy, we're going on strike and vowing not communicate with Jacky."

"Lilac, come here. I need to talk with you."

Lilac gasped and slowly walked towards Jacky as if she were in a trance.

"I have two plane tickets for you and Daisy. Gather your clothes just for the summer, before you know it…"

"So, we are not living there forever?" said Lilac.

"No, you will be back home when summer ends. Lilac, you know, despite what you think or feel about me. I love you, my little lily. I know I have not been the mom you see on television, but those women are not real. I have real love for you and Daisy. You are so much like me. I do not know if that is good or bad? I promise when you see me again. I will be a better human being for Christ's sake."

"Jacky, let me go. You're squeezing the life out of me."

"Daisy, come here. I see you peeping from around the corner."
She paused, taking in the moment. "Lilac and Daisy, I need you to
be in your best behavior."

"Come on, Daisy. Let's start packing our clothes. The sooner,
the better. And remember, we are heading to a better place, and a
better life in California. The more I think about it, Daisy, I cannot
wait to leave this house. I love Jacky, but watching her sell drugs and
pay less attention to you and me are really getting on my nerves."

As the girls packed their belongings, Jacky softened the mood
by playing Frank Sinatra's "My Way." Jacky stood outside Lilac and
Daisy's room, listening to her oldest daughter take leadership.

"Daisy, fold the underclothes separate from your jeans and
shirts," said Lilac. "I promise to look after you and teach you how
to be healthy. Listen to only me. Do you hear me? We do not know
them, people. Our mother is extremely sick and is a broken woman."

"What if they do not have the same color skin as we do, Lilac?"
asked Daisy.

"Daisy, I don't care what color those people are, I told you, you
are not Black at all! Don't ever forget that in California." Skin color
is major, in this racist-ass country.

"Bravo! Exceptional performance, Lilac," said Jacky. "Teach
your sister to take the skin that she was born to be privy of and be
happy, that she's not dark-complexioned matters seriously. No, we
are not Black, Daisy!

"Daisy, go look at yourself in the mirror and tell me what you
see."

Daisy shrubs her shoulders and softly mumbled, "White."

"Satisfactory answer! Look, my little lily, let me help you out
a bit. You are White! You have no Black features whatsoever. So be
proud," said Jacky!

"Hell, your father was the same. He is somewhere living his life
passing with his women of purity. I was not good enough for him, or
should I say pure and sufficient to marry. I was only good enough to
birth his beautiful children that he chose to abandon in this horrible
world," said Jacky. "He left me alone to raise you. I am doing my best
and gave you the best I can give.

"Sorry to say, Daisy's skin color does matter wherever you go in this world. We are not the only people passing in this millennium. Play your cards right, and as you get older, Daisy, you will appreciate the education of what your sister and I are providing.

"Don't ever speak the truth on the blood that runs in your veins. When you get older, marry or date men that are white as snow. With a good family foundation, long old money, and treats you like Queen Charlotte of Mecklenburg. When you get to California, you will be able take trips all over the world.

"Lilac and Daisy, you both are my soon-to-be queens, my dear daughters. Daisy, my cute little quiet flower. I do not want you to go through life blind. You are never too young to know your worth. One day you will look back and thank me for the joyous occasion of sending to off for the summer."

"Since we are only going for the summer, we do not have to pack much," said Lilac.

"To be honest, my little lilies, everything you have here can be replaced. Do not pack much."

CHAPTER 4

Grand Climacteric

"COME, GIRLS. WE'RE ALL PACKED. Let us get some rest before the sunshine."

Jacky left Lilac and Daisy's room; the girls felt a moment of relief. They began to pillow talk and recall about the good times they had with their friends and how much they were going to miss them and Washington DC. The girls laughed themselves asleep at the sound of Go-Go that played in passing cars.

The sun rays were beaming across Jacky's face through the torn dingy lace curtains. She opened her eyes and jumped grabbed her robe.

"Lilac and Daisy, wake up! We overslept! Hurry to wash up, and brush your teeth!" said Jacky

Lilac rolled over and woke Daisy in the full-sized bed they shared. Daisy started to cry but move slowly towards the bathroom.

"Put some fire in your step, girls, before we miss our flight."

"We're moving as fast as we can, Jacky!"

Face tight like a closed tulip, Lilac asked Jacky, "Why do you keep saying we? Are you going with us, Jacky?"

"Oh no, my little lily. I am not going with you. It is just a figure of speech. We will always be one no matter where you are. Come on, girls. I arranged for someone to take our bags downstairs."

As the girls got dressed, Jacky brewed herself a fresh cup of coffee and fired up a cigarette, exhaling as if it was giving her the mental concentration to complete this moment.

Lilac and Daisy started to choke!

"Jacky, can't you see we are allergic to cigarette smoke? We are choking. Please put it out," said Lilac.

"Okay, are you two finished putting on your clothes?"

"Yes, we are ready, and still clearing the smoke from our faces, can't you see that?" Daisy had stopped crying and was beautifully dressed, and so was Lilac. They were ready for their flight.

Knock, knock, knock.

"Who is there?"

"It's Mr. Quincy."

"The door is open. Come in," Jacky responded. "The luggage is in the back. Thank you for helping us out."

"The cab is on its way! Come, girls, let's go."

"I'll hold the door for you, Mr. Quincy," said Lilac.

"Where are you going?"

"To our aunt's house in California for the summer."

"The summer?" Mr. Quincy replied.

"Yes. We'll be back soon right before school starts," said Lilac.

"Have an excellent time and lots of fun! I will make it my business to see you when you get back. I will still be here helping your mother curry her bags up the steps."

"Thank you, Mr. Quincy. You are so lovely to Jacky and us. We are going to miss you."

"Come, girls. Here is our taxi!"

"Hello, ma'am, where are we going?"

"National Airport. There is an eleven o'clock flight we need to board."

"Yes, ma'am," said the driver. He jumped out of the yellow cab and grabbed the luggage from the curve and threw the luggage in the trunk. "All set. Let's go, pretty ladies. We should be there in no time."

The driver reached in the compartment and gave both girls a lollipop. It was cherry, their favorite flavor. "Here you are, young ladies; it breaks my heart to see sad faces. This will make you smile."

"They ought to be thankful I am sending both to California for the summer. I do not understand these children nowadays."

The driver looked straight ahead as if he could not relate to Jacky.

*****

"We are here! I hope you have an excellent time in California. Let me get your suitcases for you out of the trunk."

"Thank you, sir, for your generosity," said Jacky. She rolled her eyes and said to "have an enjoyable day on purpose, you old piece of shit!"

"Lilac and Daisy, we have a few minutes to meet this flight. We do not have much time to talk because we overslept. I love you. Hug me. I will call you the minute you arrive."

"Bye, Jacky. We love you and see you in September!"

The stewardess went with Lilac and Daisy to their flight. Holding Daisy's hands tight as ever, Lilac whispered to Daisy, "Are you scared?"

"Nope! I am happy, Lilac. We get to live in California for the summer!"

"Yes," the girls screamed with laughter, running down the ramp of the airplane.

"Calm down, little ladies. Watch your step, Lilac and Daisy," said the airline stewardess.

"Stand right here, said the stewardess. "Well, you little ladies are in for a treat. You are flying first class!"

"What is that?" Lilac asked.

"You get the absolute best of everything while flying to California. Sit back and keep each other company. I will watch over you along the way."

"What kind of mother would put her children on a plane by themselves?" said Lilac. "When I grow up am going to pay Jacky back! I wonder if there's any more surprises. You know, Daisy, some-times it feels like an adult."

*****

Lilac and Daisy woke to gentle taps on their shoulders.

"Wake up, little ladies. We're due to land in a few minutes."

Lilac and Daisy stretched in their seats, wiping their eyes.

"We're in California?" Daisy asked.

"Yes, sunshine."

"Who's going to get us? Do we stay at work with you?"

"No, sweetie. I'm getting ready for my next flight. Your relatives are here to pick you up."

The stewardess embraced Lilac and Daisy. "I am going to escort you and your sister to meet your family, Jade. She is just as sweet as your mom. Your Aunt Jade and your Uncle Jack own a large beautiful home in Santa Barbara, California.

"There's enough room for you. They have a built-in studio with a stage. Maybe Aunt Jade will make a star of both of you. Let's go; we don't want to keep them waiting."

The three of them walked as fast as they could through Santa Barbara Airport. As they approached the gate, Lilac could see her rel-atives. They looked just as she envisioned them on the flight.—Jade with the looks of Jacky and a middle-aged gentleman with dark hair and the same eyebrows as Jacky. There they stood arms wide open.

"Lilac and Daisy!" they shouted. They both ran as if there was a magnetic force that pulled them to Jack and Jade.

"Aunt Jade and Uncle Jack!

Jade hugged the stewardess and called her by her name, Mamie. "We can take it from here."

"No problem, Jade and Jack. See you soon or call me if you need it."

"Thank you. You've done enough."

"Lilac and Daisy, we have so much for you to do," said Jack. "How was your flight?"

"Are you our aunt and uncle?" Lilac didn't waste any time. "Jacky said we are going to stay with our aunt and uncle?"

"So you don't know your grandparents?" said Jade.

"It's a big secret, but to answer your questions, we don't know who our grandparents are," said Lilac.

"I know your grandparents; you are looking at them," said Jack.

"I am so shocked and happy at the same time. We finally meet Jacky's mother and father! Jacky told us an enormous lie; she said her mother died from old age. She said we are staying with our aunt and uncle for the summer. All she ever does is lie to us," said Lilac.

"I wonder where she gets that from," said Jade. "We always taught our daughter to tell the truth. But don't call us Grandma and Papa. We prefer to be called by our birth names, Jade and Jack. Like you are Lilac and Daisy."

"Now I'm confused," said Lilac. "No one seems to own up to their titles in this family. Jacky doesn't want to be called Mom, and our grandparents do not want to be called by their generational titles, Grandma and Grandpa."

"I see you have a spicy mouth… Mind your manners, little one," said Jade. "You must be hungry. We have prepared meals for you at home. I know you don't know us well, and that's with no wrongdoing on my and Jack's behalf."

"Jade! These are children be gentle with them," said Jack. "The limousine driver is waiting on us; we are late by fifteen minutes."

The limousine driver waited, parked. The family joined hands and walked towards the curb where the limousine was parked. The limousine driver got out to greet everyone, with a gracious smile on his face.

"Good afternoon, Mr. and Mrs. Chad. I see you finally have your little ones!"

"Yes," Jade happily replied. "They will be with us for a while. I have been working years around to prepare for this day. Mason, meet Lilac and Daisy."

"Pleased to meet you, misses. My name is Mason. I have been working with Jade and Jack for thirty years."

"Wow! Thirty years, that a long time, Mr. Mason."

"Giving God all the glory, I am so thankful the spirit brought you to me. Now I can see you run across the lawn through the lilies filled with honeydew flowers, butterflies, and night bugs that glow in the dark. We will be able to see you two girls grow up to become beautiful inspired by your surroundings."

"Just like my daughter named after me," said Jack.

The girls could not help but wonder and intake all the beauty Santa Barbara had to offer while riding in the limousine. It was a much distinctive look from the ruined burned down businesses of Northeast Washington DC.

"It looks like you are rich," said Lilac. "Look at the beautiful hills, and rich scenery of California. I am glad Jacky sent us here to be with you for the summer! I cannot pretend to be remedial and fake emotions, this place is beautiful," said Lilac. Jade gave notice to Lilac vocabulary.

Mason slowed down the limousine and made a right turn in the large home with palm trees, pool, basketball court, play area, and a huge driveway.

Lilac grabbed Daisy's hand as Mason stopped the vehicle. Lilac popped the doors with Daisy in hand and screamed, "We're rich!"

"California is so beautiful!" shouted Lilac.

Daisy ran around and plopped in the plush grass that stood high like four inches of carpet.

"We have one more major surprise for you after you eat dinner, my little flowers," said Jade.

Lilac and Daisy began to take in all their surroundings.

Lilac softly whispered to Daisy, "Did you hear what Jade said, Daisy?"

"No, what did she say?"

"Jade said we would be here for a long time."

"I didn't hear her say that," Daisy replied.

"Well, I did," said Lilac.

"At least she has the common decency to tell us after we eat," said Daisy. Daisy stared at Lilac with a look of "This cannot be happening again."

"I bet it's something dreadful to discuss, just like Jacky did at the last supper," said Lilac.

"Just think, Daisy. Isn't it strange that Jacky did not come and meet her parents?"

"Come on, my little flowers, dinner is now served."

Lilac and Daisy never saw anything so beautiful. The table was so decorative and with the paintings of Jacky, the family, and three other relatives they were yet to meet.

Lilac and Daisy began to eat shrimp, filet mignon, and asparagus. They'd never had either. They slopped it up as if they were in a concentration camp. Jade and Jack began to walk towards the table and grabbed the seat alongside Lilac and Daisy. They both stopped eating and looked at Jade and Jack.

"What we do?"

"Lilac, nothing is wrong. You've done nothing to no one," said Jack. "We love you with all we have. There is something we both need to tell both of you."

"Knowing your mom, she didn't tell you the truth," said Jade.

"What is it, Jade?" Lilac asked.

"You will never return home to your mother," Jade gently said.

"What are you talking about? Jacky said we stay here for the summer."

"Lilac and Daisy, you were unknowingly adopted by us."

Lilac jumped up from the table and screamed, "Adopted! Excuse me, granny, what the hell are you talking about? My sister and I are going home at the end of the summer. Call your daughter Jacky!"

"Young lady, who do you think you're talking to? I am not your mother. I am someone that can give you a better life. I understand you are upset, but don't ever disrespect me in my home if you are breathing. You got that?" said Jade.

"Lilac, please calm down. I'm relieved and happy of the announcement by Jade and Jack. You should be too. Look at the conditions we were living in," said Daisy.

Lilac began to weep. "Is there anywhere I could go lie down?"

Jack got up and picked Lilac up and carried her to the family room. He sat Lilac down on the couch and told her everything was going to be all right.

"Jacky should be calling soon. Here's some tissue. Dry your eyes, sweetness."

Jack sat across from Lilac to give her assurance that she has his full support.

The door opened in the huge foyer, and in came three more family members.

"Hi, Lilac. My name is Ava."

"Mine's Sammy."

"And I am Theodore. We are your aunt and uncles."

Lilac began to reflect on the paintings in the dining room.

Sammy—wearing black pants, a black shirt, and a roman collar—said to the crying ten-year-old Lilac, "Why are you crying? Cheer up. Everything is going to be fine. You are going to love living here. You've gained me as your big brother and protector."

"I miss my mom, Jacky."

Ava walked to Lilac and stooped down to Lilac and hugged her, not saying a word.

"It's going to be okay. Here," said Sammy with a seedy stare.

"Mind your business, Sammy! She was not talking to you," said Ava.

Theodore was the same age as Lilac. He was accommodating and pleasant.

"Come, Lilac. We can play outside. Let go swimming!"

"I must get my sister, Daisy. She's at the dinner table with Jade."

"Let's go. We're going to have so much fun swimming. Finally, I have someone to talk to that is young like me," Theodore replied.

"Hi, Jade. Can Daisy and I go swimming in the pool with Theodore?"

"Of course. Go to your rooms. We have plenty of clothing for both of you."

"What's your favorite color?"

"Lavender."

"And what's your beloved color, Daisy?"

"Pink."

"Thank you, Jade, for thinking of us," said Lilac.

Jade immediately knew what Lilac was referring to—the adoption. Jade knew not to respond to the Jacky that dwelled inside of Lilac.

"Have fun, girls. We have fresh lemonade for every dry mouth! Enjoy your swim. And, Theodore, no horse playing and take care of your nieces."

"Enjoy your swim."

CHAPTER 5

Poison Ivy

LILAC AND DAISY WOULD FALL fast asleep. Suddenly, in the middle of the night, Lilac would feel a tug at her leg and touch on her forehead. It was Sammy, motioning for her to get out the bed. Lilac was confused. She jumped up and stared in fear. Sammy stood in the shadows of the door, motioning with his hands for Lilac to come and follow him. Lilac was too young to fathom what was going to happen to her next.

Sammy took and pulled Lilac into his room and told her to "lie across the bed and take your panties off." Sammy undressed and thrust his twenty-year-old body onto the ten-year-old helpless Lilac. She began to cry; he covered her mouth and penetrated the helpless ten-year-old Lilac. Blood began to fill the sheets from the ten-year-old child.

Jacky, help me, Lilac cried aloud in her head. She was too petrified to scream! The excruciating pain of the penetration from her uncle-brother Sammy caused a lion to *roar* inside of Lilac. She began to fight Sammy! With one hand free, Lilac reached the nightstand, grabbed the crystal lamp, and cracked Sammy as hard as she could on the head!

"Awhhh, you little bitch!" screamed Sammy.

Lilac jumped up and ran through the mansion, blood trickling down her little legs, heartbeat racing and pounding, hardly able to breathe! Lilac ran and turned the doorknob straight into her grandparents' bed!

As her foot crossed her threshold, Jade screamed, "Lilac!"

The badly sexually abused ten-year-old little girl screamed for her mother Jacky, crying pitifully, mucus running down her narrow nose, wearing her favorite pink nightgown, and a bloody mess.

Jade screamed, "Lilac! My baby, what happened to you? Why are you bleeding?"

Jade reached for her nightstand and realized the blood stains on Lilac's gown! Jade grabbed Lilac and hollered for Jack! Tears began to stream down her face; she was apprehensive and nervous of what happened to Lilac!

"Who did this to you?"

Lilac, flustered and body filled with pain, became mute. Lilac was too afraid to speak of the violations and lifetime trauma that was forced upon her.

Jade screamed like a knife was jammed in her back and ran to her closet to get her guns, as the one in her nightstand was not enough to kill the perpetrator.

"Oh my god, one of you heartless sons of bitches did this to this baby!" screamed Jack. "I am going to kill one of you!"

Theodore and Ava rushed to the aid of their parents.

Sammy was trying to hide the crime scene in his room, trying to dress as quickly as possible to flee the scene.

Jack kicked Sammy's door and approached Sammy. "How could you do this to a child! A cleric!"

Jack grabbed Sammy and punched him in the face, grabbed the same bloody lamp, and cracked him on the head! Sammy dropped down to the floor like a puppet!

Jack and Jade both pulled their guns out on Sammy, staring him down in his evil eyes.

"How could you do this, Sammy, stripping Lilac off her girlhood? You are trifling, low-down, dirty, good-for-nothing son of Satan!"

Ava went to console Daisy; she was still sound asleep during all the commotion. Ava lay down Lilac's bed filled with sorrow for Daisy's big sister, Lilac.

Theodore screamed, "Jade and Jack, please do not kill him. He's still my brother!"

Theodore stood in madness and disbelief of the heinous act his older brother, the soon-to-be cleric, committed against Lilac.

They began to shout, "Why couldn't you get a woman your age? She's a child!"

"Sammy, you have a girlfriend, Madeline, that's twenty years old! Guess she not young enough," replied Theodore.

Theodore, crying unmercifully and in disgust, screamed to Jade and Jack, "You need to put him out!"

Jade pointed the gun in Sammy's face and said, "He can't stay here. No son of mine will claim fame in this household as a child rapist."

"Pack your clothes and get out of my house," said Jack. "Leave whatever belongs to you, leave it behind. Love no longer resides in this household for you."

Jack pointed the gun in Sammy's face before escorting him to the garage.

"Jade, I did not touch that girl. She's trouble, just like her mother!"

Jade, still holding the gun, said, "Sammy, if you do not get your shit and get out of my house now before I unleash a hell of gunfire on your Black ass… Jack, get him out of here before I commit a Jimmy Hoffa on his nasty, disgusting, low-down dirty ass."

"Get out before I call the police!" Jade shouted.

"I ought to punch that little girl in the face. Come here, you little bitch!"

Jack pulled the trigger and stopped Sammy in his tracks, and so did Jade.

Lilac ran and dashed into the kitchen, trying to fit into a lower-case cabinet. Jack raised his gun and hit Sammy over the head with the handle of the gun.

"Please pull the trigger, Pops," said Sammy while on his knees.

Jade ran to the kitchen to console Lilac. "Lilac, come, my dear precious lily. Grandma loves you, and I promise to make this go way."

Jack, standing over Sammy, said, "Get up. You're not worth killing for me! After what you have done to this baby, you are already dead. Get up and get out of my house. I'm leading to the garage for the last time. If you make one bad move this time, they are going to find you somewhere stinking!"

Sammy rose up slowly and turned, staring at Lilac as if she had done something to him. "You little darling little bitch, just like your mother, Jacky!"

Jack kicked Sammy in the penis floor, Jack then grabbed him with one hand, holding the gun, and pulling Sammy up of the floor with the other.

"Now we are going to try this again, Sammy."

"Jack, where I am going to go?" Sammy shouted.

"You should have thought about that before you let the devil take control of your mind. Go before you die tonight! You are banished from this family forever."

Sammy, filled with rage, said, "Jack, I have nothing or nowhere to go."

"Get off my property before something bad happens to you, son."

Sammy got in his car. Jack opened the garage to let Sammy out of the estate.

Sammy drove off and taunted Jack as he drove out of the garage. "You should've killed me, Jack. She isn't the only one I took advantage of."

Jack stared in disbelief and was mystified of Sammy's statement. Jack could not let Jade know of Sammy's last words to him as he left the garage.

Jack rushed back into the family room where Jade, Lilac, Theodore, and Ava stood. Lilac was in the arms of Jade with Ava seated close beside her. Jack and Jade communicated with their eyes, acknowledging the facts that Sammy was gone. Jack picked Lilac up as she was helpless in Jade's arms and laid her in the Wellness Room.

"Everything is going to be all right, Lilac." He could only bring comfort by words at this moment.

27

CHAPTER 6

Yarrow

THERE LILAC LAY, LOOKING INTO the air as if God was coming to scoop her up, wishing death for herself, and wondering what she did to make Sammy attack her.

Why and what was happening to me...? I want Jacky...

A soft knock came upon the door. It was Dr. Braque and his wife, Ann, who was a pediatric nurse. They both walked in the Wellness Room in angelic formation.

"My sweet dear, let us make you feel better. We need you to undress. Do not worry. We are not here to hurt you."

The ten-year-old child lay battered, bruised, and confused. Lilac had an out-of-body experience, as if her life had transcended to Jacky's arms in Washington DC.

The doctors took a quick glance at her vagina. "She has bruises."

Lilac said nothing, scared of the threat that Ava told her. "You better not tell nobody, not even your mother, or you won't be allowed to come back with Daisy."

Lilac kept her mouth shut to protect her little sister, Daisy. The physical and mental damage had been done. Lilac could not bear the thought of her sister being violated.

Dr. Ann and Dr. Braque never asked Lilac what happened or who did it. Dr. Ann asked to put some ointment on Lilac's vagina area, inserted a mini pad inside her panties, and connected Lilac to the I.V.

Lilac lay in silence, in discomfort, gazing into the shining lights in the ceiling of the Wellness Room to help her fall asleep.

"Where is Daisy?" said Lilac.

"Daisy is still asleep," Jade replied. "Lilac, my sweet, please don't worry about Daisy. She's safe with Ava in her bed, sound asleep."

In Lilac's subconscious mind, she would remain her sister's keeper and protector forever.

Amaryllis

"Doctors Ann and Braque, thank you for rushing over to help. How could we ever repay you?"

"Please don't worry about that right now, Jade. You have enough on your hands—a wounded child. She has a lifetime ahead of her. Jade, you have no idea how this will affect Lilac's future. She is an incredibly beautiful girl, how could—"

"Don't utter his name in this house anymore!" Jade turned away from Dr. Ann.

"Jade, at some point, Jack and you must come up with a plan of care for Lilac, poor child. I am certain she will need a medical team that will help her to push through this tragedy."

"What do you suggest?" said Jade as she slowly turned around. "Dr. Ann, I'll hire you double the amount that you are getting paid now."

"What? Jade, I love to work with you, but it's more important that I help as many children as I can. I cannot imagine—"

"You can't imagine what? Making more money than you are making now? I don't understand, please show what I missed, my dear friend."

"Jade, since you insist, I'll come every evening after work to help until you can get a trusted team to help her suppress this dreadful scene."

"Ann, you have no idea what this means to Jack and me. Thank you for helping and coming to our call for help. We trust that you have this as personal information."

"That is correct," said Dr. Ann.

"Of course. Please, this is confidential. What happened here tonight will remain a family secret," said Dr. Ann.

"Thank you. I could not be more grateful, Ann. Since we are having this trusting conversation, sign this NDA."

"A nondisclosure agreement? Really? When did we get here, Jade?"

"We got here the moment you decided to come and aid our situation! Dr. Ann, you know how this town is only twelve inches in width and length. Besides, it is not as if you've never signed an NDA for yourself of who your child's father is… Remember that?"

"Hush! Hand me the document."

"Dr. Ann, get Dr. Braque in here to sign his John Hancock."

"Here, sign this document."

"What document?"

"A nondisclosure agreement."

"What type of madness is this, Jack?"

"You know our reputation is all we have in this town. One must protect it with their lives," Jack replied.

They both looked at Jack and Jade and nodded their heads; the couples gave each other a firm hug of reassurance that Lilac's secret was safe with them.

"Thank you for coming. Let us know if you need anything, no matter what the cost. You've done so much for us and our children."

"It was a no-brainer to come. Try to get some rest."

"Jack, what are we going to do about Lilac? How do we deal with such?"

"Jade, calm down. We are going to hire the best care in Santa Barbara."

"Maybe hypnosis?" said Jade.

"That does not sound like a bad idea. Maybe down the road, but right now it's too far-fetched. Let's go and rest up with Lilac. She needs us more than anything."

"You're right."

CHAPTER 7

Diversion Lily

LILAC HASN'T AWOKEN FROM THE shock of Sammy forcing himself on her in a long time. Lilac woke up five years later from the trauma of Sammy forcing himself upon her. Jade ran over to Lilac's bedside, hoping she didn't remember anything and so happy to see Lilac awake from her induced coma.

Lilac jumped up as if nothing had happened.

"Daisy…"

Lilac attempted to rise from her bed but her legs were shaky. Jade's home-care nurse rushed to her bedside to ensure she didn't not move around much.

"Who is this lady? What's going on?" said Lilac.

"You fell down from off the fifteen-story banister," said Jade. "Don't you remember?"

"I don't remember anything. I'm not sure what happened to me. How long have I been sleeping? Did Jacky ever call Daisy and me?"

Lilac started to observe the health care technician that was seated in the Wellness Room and all the medical instruments around her.

"Jade, where is my little sister, Daisy?"

"She went with Ava to Aruba for the rest of the summer."

"What? Who told you to send my sister off?"

"She is fine, Lilac. I promise you."

Lilac remembered nothing of the unfortunate circumstances that put her into the Wellness Room; she was bewildered, and Jade loved every minute of it.

"I have a surprise for you, pretty girl! Jack and I are going by our generational titles Grandma and Papa! How you like that, Lilac?"

"I love that, Grandma. Finally, someone that I can call Ma."

"Yes, my dear. I don't want you to get out of bed just yet. You've been sleeping for quite some time. It's going to require physical therapy."

"I really tripped myself up, Grandma, didn't I?"

"No, you can do no harm in my eyes."

"I'm not hungry, only tired. I'm going back to sleep. Can I get up and call Daisy tomorrow?"

"Sure, she is going to cry tears of joy to see you awoke."

"Thank you, Grandma. Can I tell you that I love you?"

"You can tell me that as many times as you like, Lilac. I could never get enough love from my favorite granddaughter."

"Thank you, Grandma."

"Now get some rest, little sugar. See you in the morning." Jade kissed Lilac on the forehead and tucked her in for the night and exited the Wellness Room, heading towards their bedroom.

Suddenly, the phone rang. Jade motioned to the maid not to answer. "Let me get it, the phone."

"Hello?"

"Hi, Jade. It's me, Jacky!"

"What are you doing calling this time of night five years later?"

"Look, Jade, where are my children?"

"What children? You gave them up for adoption, now you want them back? You must go through ten presidential elections before I give them back to you! Get off my line before I take what little you have, peasant."

Click... She suddenly heard the dial tone.

Jade started thinking of the betrayal and heartbreak Jacky caused by running off with Stephen, the love of her life. The restless relationship caused Jade and Jacky to separate and live in separate ends of America. The resentment was so clear that California wasn't big enough for them both. The affair resulted into the birth of Lilac and Daisy.

"She has some nerve. They are mine now, and I will do everything in my power to protect and provide. Asking questions will be secondary in comparison to nothing. These are my lilies," said Jade.

"It was five years ago that Jacky had decided to leave her kids in our care."

Jade's head was thrown by fractions of a second by racing thoughts, and she began to imagine Jacky's disrespectful behavior.

Five years of missed birthdays, tooth fairy, and opening presents on Christmas morning. Five years without hearing a word from her kids probably didn't pierce her heart. Jacky had reinvented herself in a new world. A world where birthday cakes and bedtime stories didn't exist. Jacky was someone else. Today the woman in the mirror was a cokehead with a habit of sleeping with men for money in the land of make-believe. Every night, chasing her high in ten-year-old, worn-down, six-inch pumps, her dreams scattered across the coke lines she would do at parties with high-powered men who just needed to feel good for the night. Jacky had experienced making others feel good just for the night one time too many. She'd gotten used to waking up in crack houses on the other side of town after a night of getting high. Broken promises and empty pockets had led her in the abyss of sex and drugs for money. Let her talk to her kids, bitch! That's dead!

"I have bigger fish to fry and appointments to keep. Let me call my renaissance man with the good wood. Hey, Dr. Rhodes, tomorrow is the big show."

"I'll be over before the rooster's call."

"Thank you. Please don't let me down."

"Have I ever? We been around the world together for over twenty years. You still married and are living the good life, aren't you, Jade?"

"Not right now, Dr. Rhodes. Let's keep this as professional as possible."

"See you tomorrow, my sweet in middle," said Dr. Rhodes.

Jade took a deep breath and said, "I'll see you then, Dr. Rhodes. Have a wonderful day on purpose."

Jade quickly ran up the dual staircase to Jack's office, nearly breaking down the doors, to inform him that Lilac awoke and had no memory of what happened.

"Jack! She's awake! My sunshine. God, thank you for saving my grace. I promise to give her my love and devotion for the rest of my life," said Jack.

Jade and Jack embraced each other as if they both just hit the lottery again.

"Jack, she was herself. No more bruising, and most important, she has no recollection of the horror."

"Every time I think of it, I killed Sammy at least a million times over," said Jack. "I often think all the money and tea in China can't take back that night."

"I know, Jack. Please let us not focus on the negative. Put our energy into Lilac and give her the best life possible. The hypnotist will be here in the morning. She will never know what's going on."

"Exactly, my dear. Jade, we better pray that we live forever. This one is so hard to come back from."

Jack asked, "When will Ava, Theodore, and Daisy be back from Aruba?"

"Some time in the morning," Jade responded.

"I wonder if five years have been enough time to ensure she is in perfect shape for Daisy," said Jade.

"I am sure everything is going to work out fine, Jade. Let's get a good night's sleep. This has been a rough five years that costs millions of dollars to keep this under wraps."

"Jack, I could not see it no other way."

"Sure, there was another way, and it was killing Sammy. That would've been a big payday," replied Jack. "I should've put him out of his misery..."

Jack was haunted by the family secret. Jack, with despair in his eyes, was hoping that Lilac would unknowingly be under hypnosis for the rest of her life.

"Good night, darling."

"Good night, handsome."

Both were thinking of their big debut in the morning when Lilac arose to get out of bed for the first time in years. They began to pray on bended knee, like a worrier, that Lilac hypnotherapy will last forever.

Night-Blooming Cereus

Lilac woke up within an hour of Jack and Jade going to sleep. Lilac started to ask the questions no one could answer.

She sat up so she could watch television. "My name is Lilac. What's your name?"

"Hi, Lilac. I'm Wafiya and I am here to watch over you until your grandmother and grandfather awake. What can I do to help you?"

"I am extremely hungry. Can you please get me some shrimp cocktail? With a dash of spicy sauce."

"Spicy sauce? My dear, I don't think that would be good for you."

"Excuse me, Ms. Wafiya. We just met, and you don't know me that well. I would like a dash of spicy sauce with my shrimp cocktail, please."

Wafiya looked at Lilac as if she wanted to slap her clear across the room as she made her exit to the enormous kitchen. "That little girl has a mouth like a pistol!" she mumbled under her breath.

Lilac had taken on a new attitude while under hypnotherapy. "I hope she knows what she is doing," whispered Lilac.

"Ms. Lilac, I have your shrimp cocktail with a dash of spicy sauce on the side. Allow me to adjust your bed before eating."

"Thank you, Wafiya. This feels fantastic. You have great mechanical skills." Lilac said, speaking as if she had been here before, it was clear from her voice. Her voice had changed; she no longer sounded like she was ten years old.

"Is there anything else you would like to have?"

"Yes, please bring me back a glass of freshly squeezed lemonade and a second serving of shrimp cocktail with my special sauce on the side. After I enjoy my delicious meal, I'll prepare for a bath, Ms. Wafiya."

"Ms. Lilac, I do not think you can get in the bath this soon. Let's wait until the morning and get the authorization from your grandmother."

"If you insist, Wafiya. Let's prepare to watch movies together. Is that all right with you, Wafiya?"

"Why, sure, Lilac. Lilac, what's your favorite movie?" said Wafiya.

"*What Ever Happened to Baby Jane.*"

"What? What happened to watching kid shows?"

"I am not a television type person, anyways. Wafiya, make yourself busy by getting me an art book or something to read."

"Sure, I will go to get those items out of the art showcase room."

"Thank you, Wafiya, for understanding my frustrations."

*****

"Wow, you overdid yourself, didn't you, sweetie?" said Lilac.

"Ha! Is something wrong, Ms. Lilac? I am trying my best to overlook your behavior…" said Wafiya.

"Wow, let's see what I should paint. Let me think."

"Why don't you paint a picture of your grandmother and grandfather?"

"That's a great idea! Do you mind turning on some music? I would like to hear a little Mozart."

"Whatever your little mind desires, Ms. Lilac."

"Why do you keep calling me Ms. Lilac? I'm not a grown woman. Please drop the miss, or you're fired!"

"Lilac, I have no way to answer that other than just being polite."

"I would like to think that is what you're doing. Anyways, thank you, Wafiya."

Wafiya turned on the Mozart, sat in the giant reclining chair, and went fast asleep. As she slept, Lilac got out of the bed and went to the stationery room where there were more art supplies and bigger canvases. Lilac got the biggest canvas she could carry and made a second trip to get the easel. Lilac began to paint a beautiful image while Wafiya slept.

The sounds of Mozart made Lilac's hands move as if she was the conductor of a symphony and the oil paint was her crowd. She was painting as if she was born with a brush in one hand and paint in the other. She was a natural. She was very composed while painting, without wasting a drop.

"The illustration is picture-perfect for Jade and Jack," Lilac whispered after completing the image.

Lilac went into her room and gathered her undergarments, took a nice warm bath, got into her new set of pajamas, and went to sleep.

*****

The rays of the sun beamed through the window of the Wellness Room, gleaming on Wafiya's face. She began to open her eyes and stretch and, at once, got up and looked at the painting. Wafiya sighed and started talking to herself.

"Lilac has talent. She's an artist. This art can sell in any art show for millions."

Wafiya was so mesmerized by the beautiful painting she didn't notice that Lilac was absent from the bed. Lilac softly walked into the Wellness Room and startled Wafiya.

"Oh my. Where are you coming from, young lady?"

"I slept in my bed and took a nice warm bath, Ms. Wafiya."

"Lilac, in the future, please don't hesitate to wake me up and let me know what you are doing to yourself. I don't want anything to happen to you. Who taught you how to paint?"

Before Lilac could explain anything, Jade and Jack entered the Wellness Room.

"Good morning, Grandma and Grandpa."

"Good morning, sunshine! How are you this morning?"

"Look at my beautiful painting. I got up and out the bed while Wafiya was sleeping and went into the stationery room and pulled out the biggest canvas and easel I could find. I could think of no one other than Jacky."

Jade and Jack first gave Wafiya a nod and hid their emotions, walked over to the table, and noticed the picture was just as beautiful as the live version of Jacky! Jade looked in disbelief as if someone had hit her in the windpipe. Jack was overwhelmed with joy of Lilac's ability to overcome while under hypnosis!

"Lilac, what made you choose your mother as the image you want to see?" said Jade.

"It's plain and simple, Grandma. That's your daughter before she's my mother."

Jack and Jade, thriving of each other's emotions, hinted something was not right and that they lost their precious little Lilac forever. The hypnosis made her suppress the horror, but it took her young soul!

At this same instant, Jade's face was carved out of stone.

"Jade, what exactly is the problem?" Jack inquired. "Jacky is our firstborn child. Why aren't you delighted to see our granddaughter create such a beautiful portrait of her mother?"

"Jack…I do. I am still shocked that Lilac overcame so much in one night."

"One night! It's been five long years filled with mental anguish, anxiety, pain, and suffering. Pull yourself together, Jade."

*****

"The next Picasso or Van Gogh will emerge in this town, and I intend to be the first. Who knows what will happen? Perhaps I'll end up marrying a producer from the movies."

"Why not a movie star?" Daisy asked.

"Because the producer is the only individual who has access to all of the funds. He pays the movie star, little sister."

"You sound a lot like Jacky, Lilac. Is this the voice you've been using since the fall?"

"I think so. There is nothing I could do about it."

"Come here, Lilac. I adore you to the core of my being. When you came back from such a severe setback, you proved to be a genuine asset to the team."

"Aunty Ava loves you. Come and give me a hug."

As Lilac approached Ava, she took her time and embraced the affection. "Because of some sort of fall that I don't recall, I was awakened from my coma, as whole five years later; with pubic hair, breast, and my voice is different… I have no recollection of any of it." Lilac began to cry a river of tears, looking out of the window, gazing at the lilac tree planted outside her bedroom window.

"No, Lilac. Don't do this to yourself! I promise I'll make it up to you. You are aunt's wildflower, so beautiful and confused."

"Confused? I am heartbroken. Let's not get it twisted nor that mysterious ass fall."

"Sweetheart, you were sleepwalking and fell off a fifteen-foot staircase. Please be thankful that you are you are breathing."

"I'm astonished by the revelations of what happened to me…"

"Lilac, I've noticed that your voice and demeanor are similar to my sister's since the fall. I'm referring to your mom."

"Aunt Ava, it feels as if I transcended into another dimension or had some type of out-of-body experience."

"It's okay, Lilac. We need a little fire in this big old house occasionally."

Ava and Lilac began to laugh.

"Aunt Ava, I must get in the shower. Thank you for taking care of my Daisy. I love you."

"I love you more, Lilac."

Mysteries

Ava was anxious to get to Jade's private suite three doors down from the master bedroom.

"Jade," she whispered harshly. "Did you hear Lilac's voice?"

"Yes, I did, and I'm not ready for it, so let's not talk about it right now. There is a lot to take in and a lot happened. Be careful about what we are talking about around her. I don't want 'it' to wake up. Now go play in your contact book, Ava."

"Well, who pissed in your coffee, Jade? Your dear, sweet, kid-loving son. A complete disgrace for generations to come.

"You won't be able to make this one up, Jade. How long do you and Jack think you'll be able to hide the truth? Every time I think of it, it makes me want to do something I never thought I would do," said Ava.

"Well, if you see him, do it for me, daughter."

"You gave him everything and look what he turned out to be. How much money will you spend to keep Lilac in a daze? How much money will you spend to keep Sammy away?"

"The real question is, when are you going to get your own?" said Jade. "Let's see, you waiting on me to die? Well, take a number, baby."

"Sorry, it must be this way, Jade."

"I'm sorry, but you're not sorry. There isn't a better way to be than this. I raised you to be this way, and I respect your fortitude in the face of opposition. You should be aware that whatever you obtain will not shatter me. Now get out of my room, you cretinous scumbag."

*****

Jade and Ava began to walk toward the dinner table.

"Lilac, I really would love to introduce you to some of my friends," said Ava.

"You will do no such thing," said Jade. "Enough is enough. We're settling for the 'It's a beautiful painting,' but that is as far as it goes, Ava."

"It's nice to see everyone smiling," said Jack.

"I surely can't wait to go house hunting tomorrow," said Ava.

"So that's the plan to exit the compound," said Theo.

"Watch your mouth, son. Select your battles wisely. Don't ever forget that."

"Yes, sir."

"Well, before I was rudely interrupted by Theo, I thought I save us some time with the search."

"Oh, you will?" said Jade. "Where did you have in mind? Could it be another state like your sister?"

"That's too easy. We are buying the one-point-three-million estate several blocks from you. I wouldn't dare leave my wildflowers here alone!"

"Well, I can't wait to visit you, Aunt Ava," said Lilac.

"Wait just one minute, little Jacky!" said Jade.

"Little Jacky? I am nothing like your firstborn."

"Lilac, since the fall, you have been not yourself. I mean you've been more like an adult than a child. What's gotten into you?"

"Nothing is wrong with me. Something happened to me, and I'm not sure what that could be. But one day in my lifetime, I will figure it out. Until then, I'm doing the best I can, period!"

"You come back with all kinds of surprises, huh, Lilac..." said Ava.

CHAPTER 8

Emancipation Lily

EMANCIPATION LILY SEEMS TO HAVE a strategy in place. One day, I'll become a monarch of this realm and a master of perception and deception. In this family, the women aren't ready for me to join them! They've got the cash, but their thinking is so dated! That which they're lacking will be exuded from me, and more will be exposed. There is no doubt in my mind, though, that I have everyone in the palm of my hand.

Lilac was listening to Beethoven in her painting suite that Jack created for her.

"Lilac, what's on your mind? Who and what are you painting now?"

"I really don't know yet, Daisy. By the end of the day, it could be the moon and stars! Depending on how I'm feeling. What are you feeling, Daisy?"

"Like, would you rather be in a public or private setting?"

"Oh! Well, that would be private for me, Lilac. Public school was a disaster. Too many fine broke gentlemen to choose from. I want to preserve myself. So it's going to private school for me this time around," said Daisy. "Can you make this painting of me?"

"The next painting will be of you, my dear sister."

"Lilac, some of your paintings are missing."

"I sold them, Daisy."

"Wow! You are a Ballah Sistah."

"Daisy, I'm painting a picture of a big mansion, something I see in my dreams. If you can think it, you can receive it."

"A mansion? We're already in one of those, Lilac."

"You are correct, and it belongs to someone else."

"You're right about that. Well, let me get out of your way."

"Thank you, my Daisy. I need this time to finish my masterpiece."

*****

"This music feels so beautiful to my soul. I will be on my own this year at the tender age of fifteen! Acting like Jacky is an underestimation of my character. They haven't seen the best of me yet... The visit will tell it all. I have a piggy bank, and there is a whole entire world calling me! I hear the crowds chanting my name. Painting has been a refuge for me, and I'll show the world what they've been missing. That world includes Jacky's weird ass. She really has one coming."

"Lilac! Who are you talking to? I've been standing here, listening to you speak your thoughts out loud for the last twenty minutes," said Jack.

Lilac never turned around to acknowledge Jack; she continued painting, not missing a stroke.

"Well, Papa, since you heard everything, I shouldn't have to repeat myself twice. I have no ill will toward you, but I was born prepared to face the challenges of life."

"What makes you say that, Lilac"?

"I am noticeably confident that I can survive on my own. My paintings will take me around the world to meet people that are likewise. If you must know, I have been saving millions for the last three months! Capitalizing from selling my art through my lawyer whom Ava introduced me to. He's helped me to manage my accounts. The exact lawyer that will be here today to serve you and Jade my emancipation documents. I've done all my research to make the transaction as transparent as possible."

"Hmm. I don't know what to say, Lilac. I'm not sure if I should be mad or proud.'

"What's going on here? Lilac, what a beautiful painting. It's lovely," said Jade. "Did I walk in at an inconvenient time?"

"I am not sure," said Jack.

"With the unfashionable look you have on your face," said Jade.

"Jack and Jade, please have a seat. I don't want to crack your faces while standing up. At three thirty today, a lawyer will come through to deliver some particularly important documents for you to sign."

Jade looked at Jack, who began to shrug his shoulders.

"Lilac has resolved to emancipate."

"What! Lilac, what has come over you? Why? In order to seal the emancipation, you must be able to support yourself! Why would you want to leave your beautiful home! You are breaking my heart, Lilac!"

"Jade! I must take this matter in my own hands. These are the times we live in now."

"The times? My love and devotion to you, Lilac, is immeasurable and you know it!"

"Jade, you are making my heart skip a beat. Nah, just kidding. But I must be in control of my own destiny, and I need you to pull yourself together because the rocket is preparing to lift off... Venus, here I come!

"Since we are now in the book of Revelations, I think it's a suitable time to mention that I've saved millions by selling my art with the help of attorney."

"Your attorney? Where did you get this idea from?"

"It wasn't anyone's idea but my own. I did not have the proper contacts, so Ava helped me."

"After I told that bitch to mind her business, she does the exact opposite and undermines my authority. That's it!"

"Jade, that's not the case. I pushed her to do this for me."

"I don't care who pushed anything. You are too young to live on your own! Making choices to leave this house at the age of fifteen!

Let me guess, the picture of the house is yours and the attorney that's taking advantage of you!

"Too clever for that, Granny. Chill… Ava stood by my side anytime the ball was rolling around on the paper. I really don't want to argue about this, and I don't have the energy," said Lilac.

"My dear, I can't wait to see what attorney you summoned to my home. I'm sure I can buy him out, Lilac."

"No, we will not do no such thing!" said Jack.

"What are you saying?" said Jade.

"You heard me. Let her make her own way. She seems to have everything in line to make it happen. Lilac, I made my choice. I'm proud of you, my dear. Just promise me one thing. That you will never forsake me by leaving California," said Jack.

"I won't. I love it here."

Jack couldn't stop grinning; his faith in Lilac was strong, and he treasured the paintbrush she was clutching in her hand, which bought her millions.

"What about you, Grandma? Can I have your blessing?" said Lilac.

"That won't fly fast with me. I can't wait to meet this so-called attorney that I don't know in this town."

"Ms. Lilac, you have company."

"Present him some hospitality, Grandma."

"I'll do my best."

Jack, Jade, and Lilac began to walk towards the family room. There stood a slim, tall, nearly dark-skinned gentleman with pearly white teeth.

"Hi, Mr. Oats, thank you for coming today. Meet my forerunners, Jack and Jade."

"Pleased to meet you. I'm Atty. Mikael Oats from the law firm of Marshall Oats. We are in Santa Barbara."

Jade did not accept his extended handshake, which was a surprise. She gave him a long hard look before making a graceful exit.

"That leaves the three of us," said Oats.

"I suppose so," Jack stated. "I have a thick skin and am built to withstand pressure. Seating is available. Please, let's get down to business. Isn't my granddaughter a piece of art?"

"Yes, she is."

"Cut the bullshit," said Jack.

"Papa!"

"You better not put your hands on my beautiful granddaughter!"

"No, that is not the case! She's too young for me, Jack! I am very married, thank you! Please get that out of your mind, Jack. I never asked her for anything other than how she wants me to build her portfolio and realm as an artist. Her future for selling her art. That is it and that's all!"

"We both are men, and we know what men do," said Jack. "Lilac, you are a brave and strong young lady. I admire your ability and strength to carry on with little or no help. Just supporting you has been a pure blessing. Are you sure this is something you want to do?"

"Yes. Jack, please sign the documents. The sooner, the better."

Attorney Oats opened his briefcase and handed Jack the papers.

"The date is set for next week," said Lilac, "and we are already halfway through the year."

"Why so fast?"

"Jack, the painting of the house I completed today is my dream home. The first brick will be laid very soon."

Jack pulled out his personal fountain pen and signed the documents. Lilac jumped for joy!

"Thank you, thank you, thank you, Grandpa. I promise not to let you down. I wish Jade were as happy as you are."

"That is all right, Lilac. I will be there for your every need. Well, your time is up, Mr. Oats."

Jack picked up the phone and requested for Mason to escort Attorney Oats to the door. Jack stood up and extended to shake Oats's hand, pulled him close, and reminded him that *Lilac was still a teenage girl.*

"Mr. Oats, your car is ready. Please follow me."

"Lilac, you're having sex with that guy? He is more than twice your age."

"No! I would not dare lay down with someone his age. Jack, please give me some respect. My body is my temple, and I will treat it as such."

Jade entered the family room. She had been crying the entire time. "Lilac, how could you do this? For the record, you will not take Daisy with you! It is breaking my heart to see you leave, not rationalizing with anything. Hidden bank accounts and homes set to build next week! This is all too much. I pray to see it happen."

"Jade, do say that you will be here to see it all. In fact, you and Jack will have your own suite. You will be able to visit anytime you want. The desire to grow into womanhood so early is no fault of my own. It is genetics too advanced in this family. Look at Ava. She is out on her own."

"At the expense of Jack and myself," said Jade.

"I am a self-made millionaire already! You should be proud of me instead of being mad."

"I'm determined to reduce Ava to the lowest denominator for assisting you in leaving my side. Daisy will not make this grand exit with you, that is for sure."

"I cannot afford to take her with me right now. The lifestyle I'm set to live will requires more than a few millions. However, when I do get on my feet completely nestled in the ground. I will come back for my Daisy. By then, she will be of age," said Lilac. "We are going to run this town together! My beautiful sister, a few good friends, and, of course, me, Emancipated Lily!"

CHAPTER 9

Black Roses

THIS IS SIGNIFICANTLY MORE THAN I had anticipated! I am the proud owner of my very own mansion, and I am the youngest person on the street to do so! Not only did I succeed to get out on my own, but I also managed to do it alone.

My high school education even arrived one year earlier than expected. There is nothing I am still unable to accomplish! What comes next? Is it possible to change my name to the Incomparable Lilac?

"Wafiya, what do you think of me going out with Mr. Oats's son, Mansy?"

"Lilac, I do not want to get involved with none of your affairs and have you place blame on me when everything falls apart."

"You are right. I am so glad that Jade let you come with me."

"Are you afraid of him?"

"No, he is nice to me. We've never done anything. I'm not ready for that yet."

"I would hope not," said Wafiya.

"How do I look?"

"You look fabulous!"

"Thank you. I am driving myself tonight, Wafiya."

"You do not have to do that, Lilac! I can take you where you want to go."

"No, you cannot chauffeur me around town everywhere I want to go."

"If you insist, Lilac."

"Well, I do. It is time for me to go. I do not want to be out too late at night."

"What time is your date?"

"Five o'clock at Pick-A-Plate. I must head out early and meet up with one of my clients concerning a painting. I certainly do not trust some of these so-called adults."

"Neither do I," said Wafiya. "Call me when you are on your way home. I'll meet you back at the house."

Lilac walked out of the house and got into her Porsche, and off she went to Sunset Boulevard. *Let me stop at this boutique. I have time to stop and get a new pair of shoes. Perhaps I should don a different outfit. I'm a young diva, and I'm ready to take on the world! I work hard to make the most of my time here, and I want to do so to the furthest extent possible.*

"Hello, ma'am. I would like to try these Jimmy Choo, please. Size 7."

"I'll be right back with your size."

"Thank you."

"Excuse me, miss. From the Hills, I'm Miles, and I've been following you."

"What? Am I giving you my full attention? It appears to me that you are a pervert since you emerged from out of nowhere, running down on me like you've known me for a long time."

"The answer is no, I'm not a pervert. I'm a person you don't want to miss out on."

"So if you're that simple, I don't want you!"

Miles responded, "Let me help you slide those on your pretty little feet."

Stranger danger sounded in Lilac's head as she walked away.

"I insist on buying you a pair of shoes at the very least."

"Where do you live? How old are you?"

"As far as I'm concerned, you're two miles long. Miles, your mother did a great job at naming you! The way you're sifting through my personal affairs."

"Do you always talk to people like that? You never answered my question."

"I never will. Now pardon me while I pay for my own items."

"Thank you for shopping with us. See you again!"

"You're welcome." *I'm glad he's gone. In no way, shape, or form would I want a man to trail behind me. Creepy, isn't it? I'll be there in thirty minutes at the most.*

Lilac safely started the engine and accelerated away.

"Oh, this is my jam. This volume is not loud enough!"

"Ahhhhh!" Music was playing in the background and panic was written all over Lilac's face. As Miles emerged from the back seat of her automobile, her beautiful violet eyes practically burst out of her face as she gasped for air. Miles climbed into the front seat of the car with his hand over Lilac's lips and a knife in her face before driving away from the red stop red light.

"I'll take your life if you don't drive, and don't say anything!"

Lilac sobbed. "Please don't hurt me. Please, I'm begging you. I'll pay you anything you want, just don't hurt me!"

"I am not going to hurt you in that way. You'll live, bitch. Make a left and go down this road."

"Stop the car and get out!"

"Please, sir. Don't hurt me, please."

The lace dress and broken shoe heels complemented her long black hair, which was now covered in leaves and soil. Miles dragged the helpless Lilac into the woods by her feet.

"Suck my dick! You're going to have to get down on all fours and do it! Wait till you see the white meat."

Lilac began to play the part but couldn't; she rather ascend back to heaven. Miles, as he proceeded to beat and strike Lilac, also kicked her in the face and stomped on her with his large black boots until she was no longer able see; he became increasingly desperate. She had to be dragged down a steep hill of boulders. After experiencing the sensation of being unconscious, Lilac exhaled her last breath. Miles ripped Lilac's delicate lace dress and then proceeded to rape her in public! Lilac managed to get away from the calamity. She ascended to the clouds for a few minutes in order to gain a better perspective of what was going on around her. She was completely at ease and pleased in the arms of the Lord at the threshold of the heavenly kingdom. There were sparkles in the sky and blue birds swooping around, and it was really breathtaking. She was not aware of any infractions during the first thirty minutes of the session. She could hear the angels conversing with one another and giving her a tour of the heavenly realms in the distance. As she laid, dead, in a place where no one would ever be able to locate her, she thought to herself.

"LILAC!" screamed out the angel of death. Lilac awoke in a state of terror, having been beaten, bruised, and humiliated. When she realized she had been flung back into the fire from which she ascended, she burst into tears. She couldn't understand why she had been thrown back into the inferno. After a while, the sun started to set. As well as the automobiles driving by, Lilac can see and hear the water gushing down the creek. After being unable to be saved by the streetlights, the helpless adolescent wondered aloud where everyone had disappeared to. On the inside, she screamed, expecting that someone would come by and save her from the grasp of the man named Miles. But no one came. When she woke up in the middle of the night, Miles was towering over her and yelling in a low aggressive tone. Miles then mumbled in her ear, "I'm sorry, I'm sorry, I'm sorry, I'm sorry, I'm sorry. Bitch, you were no longer alive! You didn't have a pulse, did you? Bitch, you weren't even living anymore! It is beyond my comprehension as to why you have returned to life! I'm going to kill you! I'm going to put you to death, and you know it!"

He became even more enraged and began pounding and kicking Lilac even harder, attempting to murder her with his bare boots and fists while he raged on. He eventually stopped. Attempting to protect herself from further blows to the face, she curled up into a ball and begged Miles to refrain from kicking her in the head and she won't say anything to anyone.

"You, trashy little bitch, if you scream, the blood will gush from the side of your neck like that pussy of yours. I'll tell my little brother that I skinned that cat since he is so amazed by you. He has such impeccable taste. I need to shake his hand." The perpetrator ran up the hill and out the woods.

Lilac proceeded to pretend as if she was dead, taking little, teeny gasps of breath barely noticeable. Lilac played unconscious; she did not flinch. She heard him flee in her car. She counted and played dead for a few minutes and then jumped up to put on her clothes! She ran through the woods into the street, and amazingly, her car was still there. Lilac, too traumatized to think of what to do, drove as quickly as she could.

"Wafiya! My life is in jeopardy because I've been raped and then abandoned. I'm at the hospital get in touch with Jack and Jade, dial their phone number. My entire face is swollen and red from the trauma! Jesus, I beg of you! I'm in trouble, Jesus!"

"Do you know where you are?"

"I'm on the street! What happened to me? I have no idea how this happened to me." On the drive to the hospital, Lilac was pleading for help. Black, blue, and violet hues covered her face, and her eyes were crimson red. She was covered in dirt, had a broken shoe, and was pleading for assistance. Once at the hospital, Lilac nearly went into a cardiac arrest.

*****

"I need your help!" Lilac couldn't stop crying, and she yelled as loudly as she could. "Jack and Jade, someone took my temple!"

A broken Lilac wailed as she lay helpless in the hospital emergency room. Both Lilac and Jade were crying as Jack held their hands.

"Wow, take a look at my face. Just look at me, I'm no better than the average woman on the street… In the hands of a complete stranger, I was pounced upon! In the end, he got away with it…"

"He will pay for this," said Jack.

"I know what he looks like. Get me a pencil and paper!"

"Who would want to harm my wildflower?" said Jack and Jade.

"I just cannot tolerate what he has done to your beautiful face. Look at what he's done to you, my sweet child," said Jade.

"I was supposed to meet Mansy for dinner at five o'clock today at Pick-A-Plate. I stopped at a boutique along the boulevard and bought a pair of heels. A strange guy came in by the name of Miles, who made an attempt to get my attention by wanting to purchase my shoes. Then he vanished…"

"The breath will leave my body if I don't handle this tonight," said Jack. "I told that attorney to not play with me about you, and he did exactly that."

Sobbing her heart out, "There should be no place on earth for people who violate women and children. My life is forever ruined," said Lilac. "I will never leave the house alone again. Jack, take this picture with you."

"Hello, Mr. and Mrs. Chad, I'm Dr. Post, the emergency physician-in-charge. I'm sorry for what happened to your daughter. The police have been dispatched. They will be here soon."

"Call them back and tell them we don't need their services. This is an isolated situation, Dr. Post," said Jack.

"I swore an oath that I would only take medicine. In the event of a crime, we must file a report. This is my house, Mr. Chad."

"Call me Jack!"

"Since you insist, Jack. This is my house, and I will run it accordingly. I heard all about you and your wife, Jade."

"You haven't heard it all, then. Cancel that call that was dispatched!"

Dr. Post walked off to derail the officers to another rape that occurred right after Lilac's!

Jade sat outside of Lilac's room and did not utter another word; she was too heartbroken. Jack helped Lilac to get dressed. He arranged for Lilac to be chauffeured home while he and Jade drove Lilac's Porsche home.

"Jack, my heart can't take anything more! That poor child has been through enough! Did you hear what Dr. Post said? Lilac nearly lost her life, and it's a wonder she's still living."

"I'm not sure how this could have happened, but I'm going to kill that son of a bitch! I am going to Oats's house, Jade, to see if I could find out more information on his family. I'll see you soon."

"What a horrendous ordeal this poor girl has had to go through in her little fifteen years on this planet."

"I did what I thought was best for her at the time, and it was the right thing to do. When it comes to Lilac, right now, I couldn't give a damn about anything in this world after what she's been through since coming into our care. This is something I need to get my thoughts together before I lose my calm, and I won't be able to return home until this is totally handled. Get a comforter to keep you warm, dear," Jack advises Jade.

In the words of Jade, "It's going to be a very long night."

Jack backed Lilac's car into the driveway and motioned for Mason to follow him in the same direction as he was driving in.

"Take me home, Mason."

"No problem, sir."

"I suppose you heard what happened earlier today?"

"You know how news travels on the compound."

"Something got to give, Mason. I'm not going to sit back as if nothing happened, that is for sure."

"I can't blame you for anything that you bring to the table for the Oats family."

"I am glad you are a man of my standards, Mason. So glad to have you in my life, man."

"We're more than friends. We are family."

"Wait here. I will be right back out. I must change my clothes. This is going to be easy. My all-black running suit and any soft-soled black shoe will be perfect. Mr. Oats, you have met your maker, sir."

"So I have nothing to lose and everything to gain, I'm ready to take on this new task. The door will not be held open for me by Mason at this moment."

"Potholes and ruts in the road seemed so loud when I was a kid since there was no radio to drown them out. "Get me there as quickly as possible, please, and I beg of you to hurry up and do it urgently, Mason. I need you to come back to my apartment and stay there until I phone you. I'm grateful for your assistance."

"Jack, you're in the driver's seat!"

Make this left and let me out, Jack hurried along a narrow wooded path. Lilac's gorgeous face popped into his head, and he begged against hope that he would discover nothing when he got to the Oats' house. The doorbell rang every time Jack knocked on the door.

Knock, knock, knock.

"Jack, you couldn't have gotten here any sooner! Golf is on the eye. Let's make a bet?"

"Throw your number out there. I got what you need in the suitcase if you can guess the amount in it. Shit, I'll give you the whole case!" said Jack.

"Thirty thousand?"

"You're right…"

"I am riding this bliss! Jack, you've always been a man of your word! I'll have Katherine come and take that off your hands!"

"Yes! Go get her, Oats!"

"I can use the money to pay for my son Miles's college tuition. Thank you for blessing Lilac and Mansy's friendship."

"Blessings, huh. Man, I never oblige to anything, Oats. Oats, are your sons here now?"

"They are upstairs configuring a new software for one of the largest corporations, Wired Up. I am proud of them."

Jack, with a look upon his face, replied, "I bet you are. Oats, you never talked about your other son? Why not?"

"Katherine, put a French 75 together for me, hon."

"Jack, we all have our problem child, and he's ours," said Oats.

"What would you like to have, Jack?"

"I'll start off with a shot of VSOP. There is no need to prepare a meal because I won't be here long."

"Boys, come on down. I need you to meet someone. Jack, these are my dizygotic also known as my fraternal twin boys, Mansy and Miles. Come in here, boys. I want you to meet one of my good friends, Jack!"

"Thank you for the drink, Katherine. I most certainly needed this," said Oats.

"No problem," said Katherine.

"Hello, Mr. Jack. Pleased to meet you. My name is Miles. I'm a major in political science at Los Angeles University."

"My name is Mansy, the beauty and brains of the family. I finally get to meet the man that raised such a lovely daughter. Lilac loves you with everything she has," said Mansy. "I am lucky to have her in my life. She is smart, brilliant, and one day, I hope to marry her with your blessing."

Jack sat down, and everyone else sat down in the family room.

"Well, you won fair and square, Oats. Everything in the suitcase belongs to you and the family."

Jack opened the suitcase and pulled out the gun with a silencer attached. "Everyone remain calm. No fuckin' need to worry about calling anyone because all of you were so comfortable that you left your cellphone throughout your home!"

Jack pointed the gun at Miles. "Tell your brother, mother, and father what you did to my beautiful Lilac! Before I shoot you in your face!"

"I don't know what you're talking about!" said Mansy.

"I am sorry, Mr. Chad! I didn't mean to rape her, it was an accident! Please, I'm begging you!"

"Miles!" Katherine yelled in disbelief.

"Get down on your knees, Miles! Come over here and bow your head!" said Jack.

"Don't murder me! Please don't!"

"There is no need to be alarmed. I won't harm you. Everyone should now be laying on the floor."

"Mansy, you've said that you're in love with my daughter. If you truly love her, show it to me… The gun is yours to keep!"

"Mr. Chad! I'm unable to do this! This is my family—my brother, father, and mother. Do not inflict this on us! Sir, we need to call the cops!" Mansy was completely taken aback when he learned that his twin brother had raped his beloved Lilac!

"Miles!" screamed Oats. "Look at the position you put this family in. Oates got down on bending knee and begged… Please Jack spare my life, and the lives of Mansy and Katherine. Please, man, I ask you to take only his life! I beseech you!"

With tears the size of dimes streaming down his face and mucus streaming down his nose, Miles cried out, "Please understand that I did not intend to offend you. On the boulevard, I saw her automobile, and a voice instructed me to commit these horrific acts of violence against her and others."

"Can you explain what you mean by 'others'?" Katherine inquired.

"I took attention of what he said, Katherine. Can you tell me what that means?" Oats remarked.

"Your boy is a devil, I tell you! He is the serial rapist, after all! You're a good boy, aren't you?" remarked Jack, who stood with his gun pointed at everyone.

"Please assure us you are not the Sidewalk Rapist?" Katherine and Oats said in unison to their son Miles, who replied affirmatively.

"Kill me," Miles exclaimed, snot streaming down his nostrils and beads of sweat forming on his forehead. "Please do the task as soon as possible. I'd like to be relieved of my misery. Having these voices in my head constantly encouraging me to be cruel to women is something I can't bear… I despise myself. There is a lot about me that you don't know. You'd be shocked to learn that I've kidnapped children of all ages, boys and girls alike. To spit even more in your faces," says Miles.

"I despise you! Who do you think you're fooling, son?" Jack exclaimed wistfully. "I'm eager to put this entire family to rest as soon as possible!"

"Please hand over the weapon to me," Oats requested. "I heard enough of the sick sadistic—"

Bloop, Bloop! Blood splashed all over the walls and carpet as Miles was knocked to the ground.

"Oats, we brought a monster in the world! You heard our son admit to committing acts of violence towards women and children!"

"I don't know where he adopted these demonic ideas… Jack, I'm begging you to please let my family live!"

"I…I…I…lost my son a long time ago years before this day," said Katherine. "I love my sons and husband… Whatever you want, Oats," Katherine said while embracing Mansy. "Are you okay, Mansy?" said Katherine.

"Mansy, you must live with this for the rest of our lives. Vow you will never say a word to ruin the little integrity we have left in this family," said Oats.

"No! I was bereaved of both my brother and my girlfriend all at the same time! My entire life has been altered irrevocably. Are you telling me that I now have to live with the fact that my flesh and blood is a serial rapist who raped my girlfriend? Mr. Chad, it would be better for you if you killed us all. Nothing in our lives will ever be the same again after this evening! We've already passed away!"

"Be careful what you ask for, son. I'm not too far from taking all of you out! But I got who I came for. I'll let you figure how to dispose of this rotten piece of flesh you brought into this world. I do not clean up nothing but my ass! I'll turn back on your security systems by tomorrow morning, and that is midnight tonight! You, too, got a lot of work to do. Oats, I'm expecting to see you by eight o'clock sharp."

"That only leaves us with two hours," said Katherine.

"Well, it could be the other way around. Just think of that, Katherine," said Jack.

Jack waved the gun toward Mansy and told him to open the door.

"Good night!"

Jack walked out of Attorney Oats's home, leaving him and his family to clean up the mess! He moved swiftly, calling Mason to pick him up at the corner of Sampson and Wells Drive.

"Mason, hurry. I will be up the street within five minutes."

"No worries. I had a feeling you're along this way. I'm here waiting on you."

"Thank you. See you soon."

Running up through the path as fast as he could, Jack arrived within three minutes of his and Mason's conversation.

"I was worried about you for a minute, Jack."

"No need to worry about me, Mason. I'm going to be just fine. Take me back to my private place to flush this shit."

"Relax, boss man. We'll be there within a few minutes."

"Good."

CHAPTER 10

Veil of Flowers

"EVER SINCE I WAS RAPED, I have another vision that comes and goes, but it does not fit in the rape scene."

"What do you mean, Lilac?"

"I often see a man lying on top of me when I was a child. It's weird, but I know that's far from the truth."

Wafiya looked perplexed.

"The trauma has caused my brain to shift and see images of horrible things. It is like it opened a crazy part of my brain."

"I got you, Lilac. I have my licensing to help provide you with the care you need to relax your mind… It has been some time since I have given you a massage. How about after you finish this beautiful painting I give you one?"

"I would love that. You are right. I do not want to do anything to hinder me from having peace of mind."

"I cannot believe five hours has passed and you are not finished."

"Oh no, Wafiya. This one is incredibly special, and it will sell for a special price! I think I've done enough for today. Ready for your massage. Let me get in the shower, then I will be ready."

"Okay, Lilac. I'm preparing to get you good and relaxed. Warming up the massage suite."

#WafiyaSeeds

Poor child. She has no idea she will never see Mansy again. God knows I'm doing my best to keep this television off today. She will certainly break down if she hears that the entire Oats family was done off!

How can I call myself a friend when I am hiding the truth from her and, furthermore, acting just like the rest of the family? As ruthless as they are, I'm in no position to test the waters. I love life too much for that. There must be a way where I can expose the truth. Lilac is a smart girl; she will be able to put the pieces together quick! She has not lost her mind, and I see no harm in her knowing the truth. So when she gets out of the shower, I'll expose her to the news so she can really paint the truth. Better now than never, praying the hypnotherapy will last a lifetime. Lord knows this child cannot bear another domestic anything.

Praying that she will be able to accept what she learns swiftly about Mansy. God didn't give me those big boobs for nothing! I never had a chance to embrace a baby of my own. Been too busy raising this baby I never had. But she treats me like no one ever has.

I couldn't be more thankful that I met Jade through passing, and giving her everything, she needs to remain disease-free throughout her years of cheating on Jack with every married man on the block. If I was a fraction of what Jade was, I'll be a very rich woman, but I'm fine with the fifty-thousand-dollar deposit I receive from Jack every month to include the ten thousand I get from Jade and living free in the guesthouse my sweet Lilac built for me.

Lilac has no idea the power her grandparent has. Ava's house has been sold, money taken from her bank accounts, and she's now living from here to there in the hills of Hollywood.

Thought I would never see the day when Jade was pushed to the limit with her daughter's trifling-ass ways. I have no doubt in my mind that she will meet that movie producer now…in the porn industry. One thing about this town, when you have no money and backbone, you have nothing.

Ms. Lilac knows more than her Aunty Ava! Unbelievable, Ava let a fifteen-year-old beat her at her own game! Miss Momma-and-Daddy-get-me-what-I-want-now-or-else!

All the money in world cannot fix that family; it has more issues than a poor man's bank account.

I wonder how long it is going to take for Jade and Jack to realize that their sweet Theo has more honey than a beehive. The "bones" I know about Theo would send Jade into frenzy, but not Jack; he is too loving and sweet. He doesn't want to lose his only son because Sammy has no chance of making his way back without him having his head on a platter.

Theo slept with so many of the rappers, actors, and athletes he should write a tell-all and get on with his life. It should read, "EXTRA READ ALL ABOUT HOW THESE RAPPERS, ACTORS, AND BALLERS ARE BEHIND CLOSED DOORS WITH THEIR ASSES UP AND FACEDOWN!"

One would think that it's the other way around, but from what I heard about Theo, he's the dominant one. Who would've thought?

Theo, so sweet, handsome, and quiet, so fine it looks like time is standing still for him. The community has spread the word about his man parts; most women are mad that he's not turned on by their beauty and money.

It amazes me how some women can't tell when a man is bisexual and ends up marrying him and having kids.

I definitely see Theo forecast as the next Liberace!

Daisy is so beautiful, and she's dating Evan Meanings from the hit show Level Up 2022.

The only relationship that has the stamp of approval from Jade and Jack. He comes from a family of wealth and long, old Hollywood money. There's nothing wrong with mixing the old with the new in my eyes.

Nonetheless, Daisy will live unscathed from the carnage that Lilac has endured. They care for each other very much, and their bond can't be broken, and I admire that in them.

How I wish I had a sister or family that I can connect myself to. Growing up in foster care and sleeping with whoever would feed me in the morning, the world would never understand how there are so many refugees that seek refuge in the Hills as house cleaners, lovers, and mothers, living on borrowed time. Let me stop. The seed that is entangled in my DNA is telling the truth. That would scare the Chad families. I am the real party.

I'm so grateful and humble.

The best thing I could've ever done was meet Jade and steal the antibiotics for her!

A perfect mistake.

CHAPTER 11

#Rose Petals

"Loving the smell of the rose water, Wafiya. I never paid attention to how beautiful it is in here until now! The tea lights, fresh fruit, and, of course, more wine. I haven't seen the news in a few days. It's time for me to see what I missed."

"Lie in chair 4, Lilac. It will enhance your view."

"Thank you, Wafiya."

"Turn on channel 36. I need to catch what's been going on around this town."

"Okay."

"Wafiya, use the organic de-stress oils, please. I feel the need to switch up. Something that will relax me is what I need while I am facedown listening to news."

"Are you ready to get the best massage you ever had in your life?" said Wafiya.

"We have two breaking news reports! The suspect known as the Sidewalk Rapist was found dead from blunt force trauma to the upper body. A note at the crime scene pointing him out as the serial rapist that shook the Palisades community for two years! Miles Oats, the twin of Mansy Oats and son of Michael and Katherine Oats, was pronounced dead at the scene.

"Moreover, there has been a fire at 5846 Honey Toned Lane, and a family of four was trapped inside. Detectives are at both scenes, trying to put the puzzle together of how long this family knew that their son was the Sidewalk Rapist. The family of Atty. Michael Oats—his wife, Katherine, their sons Miles and Mansy were asleep as the fire was set! Investigators announced all doors were locked from an electronic system that jammed as the house was ablaze! Inhaling toxic poisoning and a faulty gas pipe that sent the house into an explosion, the entire family perished! No other victims were reported at this time. We are a community in mourning. John, back to you."

"Wafiya! Please tell me what I'm hearing isn't true!"

"It was Mansy's twin brother, Miles, that raped me? The brother I never met? Mansy always warned me that his brother was not someone I wanted to meet! *He was ashamed of him and he never told me why.* He knew his brother carried some demons, but I can't imagine he knew it was this deep The entire family dead! It explains why Mansy never called me after what happened to me! I thought he was avoiding me because of what he heard... Mr. Oats was a particularly good man and his wife, Katherine. The pain they must've endured finding out that truth of what their son became. *Oh my god,* Mr. Oats took his entire family off this earth! The fact that his son is the Sidewalk Rapist broke their hearts into million pieces. Wafiya, this is so heartbreaking. I thought..."

"I wanted you to know the truth, Lilac. Sorry but you must know the truth. I didn't want to treat you like Jack and Jade did and hide real life from you. You are like a daughter to me, and what affects you affects me too. I cannot deny what I did was wrong, setting this massage up for you to see the news. But what other way for you to find out? I wanted you to feel some vindication behind what happened to you. Lilac, it hurts so bad when I look at you. It hurts so bad, my dear..."

"I am not mad at you. How could I be? Wafiya, you have been the only woman that has been consistent in these last few years. I appreciate the truth even though this is a lot to take in! They would have kept me in the dark as long as possible. Wearing blinders is not an option. The fact is, it is tragic for all of us. The families are affected by the acts of violence Miles committed against me. He stalked me, Wafiya, for God knows how long. We never met. He just appeared from out of nowhere."

"Lilac, don't go back to that day. I want you to take this moment and feel good that he can no longer hurt another person, another child."

"You are right. I'm angry, hurt, and mad at the same time, Wafiya. It's innocence lost from an entire community, not just me… It was twenty other women and children that were victimized by Miles. I hope Jack beat him with a *shit stick* and hung him for smelling! May he burn in the pits of hell and meet his demons!" said Lilac. "I can boldly admit it feels good a little to know that he's dead, but I still had love for Mansy. Love that I will never experience again, not this lifetime. Wafiya, there is no question on how that house caught ablaze! Ha ha ha! Jack sure didn't waste any time, did he, Wafiya?"

"No, he did not. Lilac, this is no laughing matter. An entire family is dead behind one man's actions. That's the part that saddens me the most."

"Well, it saddens me, too, but it brings joy to my heart to know that my Jack did what he thought was best for me! When you mess with someone's family in this capacity, you get what's coming. As they say, 'don't bring a knife to a fistfight.' I thought I was going to die, Wafiya…"

"Lilac, you act as if you want to celebrate the death of an entire family over one sick sadistic bastard!"

"Not a celebration but more like rejoicing, if you will. I have something to be happy about. The sly, slick, and wicked is not breathing to hurt another soul. C'mon, Wafiya. I'm ready for that 'best in the world' massage you were talking about."

Tables are turning, you think…

The tables have turned for me once again in my favor! I finished my black-and-white portrait with a hint of red lipstick and my violet eyes that peeped through the lace veil.

"That sounds eccentric, Lilac. What made you think of that?"

"It captures the mystery underneath the veil. Wafiya. The veil will play an intricate detail in my daily attire even if it is in a pair of jeans, tank top, and a pair of red bottoms. Trendsetting! One thing I learned from Jack is to turn a negative into a positive. This painting will be one of my biggest contributions to myself!"

Wafiya raised her eyebrow. "Take your time and focus on one thing at time, Lilac. You know I'm not wrong."

"You're right, Wafiya, but I can talk out loud about my goals and ambitions. It's all I have right now. So let me keep it! I don't mean to come down so hard on you, Wafiya."

"I don't want you to move too fast and forget everything that you are working towards, Lilac. Please, so much has transpired in the last two weeks. Let us take it slow," said Wafiya.

"All right, Wafiya. That feels good. I can go straight to sleep. Your hands are like magic, and that brain wave music relaxes me. Sometimes I wonder if you are hypnotizing me, Wafiya."

"Don't be silly, Lilac. I don't have the capabilities to bamboozle anyone. Besides, you are too smart for that. I am here to help you, and that is it! Now enough of the bad vibes, thoughts, and feelings. Let's get you relaxed and prepared for this facial," said Wafiya. "Close your eyes and relax while I rub your temples and you Zen. Smell the sweet aroma of the rose petals. You will only attract the good in yourself and the goodness in others, Lilac. Anything in your past will not affect you in this lifetime or any other. Light, love, and life are the answer. Relax and listen to the sound waves."

"Wafiya, I'm sleepy now. Close the door."

"Rest on, Lilac. I'll wake you in time…"

CHAPTER 12

#BouquetofRoses

"The cat almost got out of the bag. That was close," said Wafiya. "This child is one tough cookie and is generous on one side and stone on the other side. She must've gotten that from her mother! Let me get Jack on the phone. I hope they are back from their ghost trip."

"Hello, Jack?"

"Hey, Wafiya. How are you and Lilac? Jade and I are holding the family together. How is my baby doing?"

"I need to discuss something with you and Jade. How long will it be before you will get back?"

"We are on our way back now. Is everything all right with Lilac?"

"Everything is going as planned. She has healed tremendously in the face with the lumps and bruising. However, the trauma has triggered other things! I don't want to talk over the phone. I don't know if this place has wires running from side to side into the ceilings to the floors, Jack."

"You are right. We will see you tomorrow, Wafiya."

"Okay, see you then."

*****

"Tonight will be a special night for my dear daughter, Lilac. Shrimp cocktail and a dash of spicy sauce will start the fire in her engine, corn on the cob boiled in milk, sugar, and butter, and a crab cake. Or maybe I will cater her a delicious meal from Pick-A-Plate. I am sure Sharee won't mind. I pray Lilac is in a good mood when she awakes. Let me do a health check. Lilac, you're up!"

"How long have I been sleeping?"

"About two hours. You had a good power nap. How are you feeling?"

"I am feeling great. A little sluggish, but above all, I feel good. What is that I smell? Is that seafood, Wafiya?"

"It sure is. I thought I'd get you one of your longtime favorites."

"Shrimp cocktail with a little bit spicy sauce?"

Lilac stretched her arms, moving her body around and around, and yawned. "Thank you, Wafiya. Let me go freshen up before I chow down on my favorite."

"Lilac, I've already set the table up Southern style so our minds can escape, even if it's just for an hour or two. Leaving the Hills of California, the city of lies and alibis."

"Wafiya, this is beautiful. No ordinary person could have pulled this off like you!"

"You are so sweet."

"Thank you so much for taking the time to show me so much love and support in the last two weeks. It's been so pure and wholesome to have your healing hands nourish my mind, body, and spirit. Whatever is mine is yours," said Lilac. "Have you heard from Jack and Jade? When will they be back? I want to finish my painting before he comes. It means so much to me, especially after what he did to heal my heart. Jack understands me and my heart. He'll get the painting as soon as he sees it."

"You and Jack have a wonderful chemistry. Don't ever take that for granted," said Wafiya.

"Never that. Just a minute, my phone is ringing. Jack, where are you guys? When am I going to see you?" said Lilac.

"We are on our way to see you and Wafiya, my dear."

"Are you bringing Daisy with you?"

"The question is, are you ready for Daisy to see you?"

"Yes, I guess so. All the bruises have healed. Wearing this veil Jade gave me has been asset. I wear them all the time now, Jack."

"It takes you to start something new. That's my girl making her way back. See you soon."

"Wafiya, you knew all the time they were home. That's why you ordered so much food! I have not seen Daisy in a few weeks. My favorite human being, my sister! She's in love now, growing up so fast! I hope she does not ask a whole basketful of questions. She normally wants me to listen to her talk about all her sneaky affairs. She's just like Jade."

Lilac and Wafiya laughed so hard.

"My, my, let me finish my painting, I want Jack to see it completed! I have at least five hours to finish up before they arrive."

"That's more than enough time, Lilac. Quickly turn on Beethoven and pull back the curtain. Let the sunshine in, please," said Lilac.

Six hours passed...

"They are pulling up the driveway now. Let me open the doors for them, Lilac."

Daisy jumped out the car; she could not wait to see Lilac!

"Lilac, we're so glad to see you! Where have you been?" said Daisy. "Making a movie or something? Why didn't you go on the trip with us, Lilac?"

"I had a lot of business to take care of, Daisy. Everything isn't handed over to us, you know."

"It can if you let it," said Daisy. "Did Jack and Jade tell you that I'm dating Evan Meanings?"

"Yeah, I heard all about it. I'm proud of you, little sister. He is a smart choice."

"Thank you. He's everything I wished for, and he makes me feel like a little queen."

"Okay, Daisy, let us get a word in," said Jade. "Honey, how are you doing?"

"I am doing great, Jade. Do not mind me. Daisy, it's good to hear great news. It is the best I have heard in the last two weeks."

"Lilac, have you been painting for any showcases lately?" said Daisy.

"I have a big project am working on now. How about I show you my *Best Contribution Ever*? That's the name of my new painting."

"Sure, Lilac. I would love to be the first person to see your painting."

"Rich girl, eat this fabulous seafood spread from Pick-A-Plate, catered by the one and only. Everyone please take a seat and enjoy the wonderful seafood feast."

"Wafiya, I need to talk to you for a few, please," said Jack. "Step out into the conservatory and chitchat and share our vacation times."

"Oh sure. I'm not sure why I didn't think of that. Lilac and Daisy, eat your heart out!" said Jack.

"Take your time," said Jade.

"These crab cakes will keep us busy!"

Conservatory of Secrets

Wafiya whispered, "The Sammy incident was nearly on the surface earlier today. She recalled a man lying on her, but I assured her it was post-traumatic, and that's it. It scared me. For a moment, I thought it was going to break Lilac! It must be in God's grace that the violation is still concealed."

"Are you okay, Jade?" said Wafiya. "You do not look like you feel too good. Where did those black marks streaming from your eyes come from," said Wafiya. "When was the last time you've seen a physician, Jade? That dry cough and red eyes?"

"Make your mind up. Do you want to be Lilac's mother? Or would you like to be mine? I'll wait..."

"The nerve of you to have any sort of bad vibe after I've been the one here to wipe her tears, hold her hand, wash her body, and love her unconditionally. You've been on your good family vacation hiding from what really happened, so let me show my girl the attention she deserves," Wafiya said. "The both of you can bring the worst out of any good situation."

"Please stop! Jade, *stop* the *foolery*! Keep your jealous heart to yourself. The woman cares about you! It's been a long hard sixty years to get the horse to the pond! This cough is kicking my ass back and forth. Shut up and let the women speak!," said Jack.

"Wafiya, stand back. I don't want you to catch this terrible cold," said Jade. "My heart can't take any more, that's all. Haven't been feeling myself lately. It was nice to get out of town and vacation in China, away from all the noise.

"Jack, my children are confused about who they are! Lilac and Daisy came into our world and pursued happiness, love, and dreams—fulfilled aspects of what Sammy, Ava, and Theodore missed! Trying to protect them from themselves has failed on a colossal level. My firstborn moved to another state, Washington DC, my second is a porn star, my son is on the down low and thinks no one knows about him sleeping with all these filthy old men, and the other a child rapist. Where did we go wrong?"

"Jade, right now is not the time for the sad songs and fucked-up movie scripts. We are talking about our sweet Lilac!"

"Well, I have nothing else left to say," said Jade.

"Good, then don't! She's preparing to showcase her painting next week with Sotheby's in the New York Museum of Art! We have a lot to be proud of. I do not give a damn how I feel…"

"I feel just as bad. Body muscles are sore from the long flight," said Jade.

"We are going to be simply fine…"

"You're right," said Jade.

"You all don't appear to be ready for Lilac's big show. She's expecting to make at least twenty-five million from this painting. Give her all the praise she needs because she is worthy of it. This child has a fire in her that a tsunami cannot put out! You two should be darn proud of her. She just cleaned it up and completed it today."

The Best Contribution Ever

"Bravo, Lilac! This is like no other! I adore this painting of you. I see the pain in your beautiful violet eyes underneath the veil. How did you manage to put the lace garment into the painting, Lilac? That is a lot of detail you put into one setting!" Jack was so wowed over Lilac's painting he shed a tear.

"It takes a little creation, a whole lot of imagination, effort, and commitment to bring your vision alive! Why are you crying?"

"Silver hair, blushed red cheeks, with sadness in his eyes... I see you, Lilac. I see you..."

"Why all the sadness, Jack and Jade?" said Daisy.

"We are not sad, Daisy. Just overwhelmed with happiness and sadness that Lilac has achieved everything and never faulting. Use your sister as an example. Resilient."

"I will... What time are we going home? I can't wait to see Evan."

Everyone laughed and gathered up their items.

"Time really flies when we're in love with one another! Five hours went by so fast. It's 1:00 a.m. Mason is waiting outside. Group hug, we love you, Lilac! Remember, we're in miles reach!"

"Have you been feeling sick too?" said Wafiya.

"No, ma'am! I keep my mask on and, of course, gloves. I have a little OCD!," said Daisy.

"Jack and Jade, promise me you will go to the hospital and get that cold medicated as soon as possible. There is a deadly disease called the coronavirus. It originated from China in a small town."

"Deadly... What do you mean by that?" said Jack. "I am going home to take a hot shower, drink tea, and have someone come and treat Jade and me in the morning."

"Promise me you'll get treatment. Don't let it manifest into something we'll regret," said Wafiya.

"Come on, you two, Mason is waiting on you!"

"After treatment is administered, call me in the morning and let me know how you are doing. I love you so much."

"All right, Momma Mia," said Jade. "I love you so much, Lilac. You have done well for yourself and your sister. If we were to leave tonight, you have it all together. Remember, *Grandma* told you first!"

"Daisy, take care of them. They have always taken care of you!"

"No worries, sissy! Get some rest. You have an auction coming soon! Good night."

"Good night, everyone," said Lilac. "Love you, Mason. Make sure you get them home safe! Text me, Daisy!"

CHAPTER 13

Amorphophallus Titanium

"WHAT TIME IS IT?" SAID Daisy. "It is 10:00 a.m. I have not heard anything from Jack or Jade this morning!"

"Good morning, Mason. Have you seen Jack and Jade?"

"No, I haven't seen anyone this morning, Daisy."

"Did anyone come to give them aid for the cold?"

Daisy ran up the stairs in supersonic speed and opened the doors to the bedroom suite. The smell of rigor mortis hit her nose. There lay the only two people who bought so much joy, love, and peace into her and Lilac's life, hugging up in fetal position.

"Jesus! Please! No! Please, God, do not do this to me!" shouted Daisy. "Jack, Jade! Mason!"

Mason dropped his cup of coffee on the floor, startled by the scream that came out of Daisy's mouth.

"Call the ambulance, Mason!"

"No, Daisy. I must go try to wake them!"

"Don't do that!" screamed Daisy. "You will become sick! Call the ambulance while I call Lilac! Close their bedroom door back, Mason!"

Mason ran to the kitchen and called the paramedics.

"Hello, 911. May I help you?"

"Please send someone to 2323 Good Wonderland Drive, Brentwood…"

"What's the emergency, sir? Please calm down. I can barely understand what you're saying!"

"My boss, my friend, my brother and sister—Mr. Jack and Jade Chad went to China and came home sick with that virus. Their granddaughter found them unresponsive! Please come help us!"

"Sir, I'm going to need everyone in the home to leave and remain outside the home while I dispatch the hazmat team to your location. Where are Mr. and Mrs. Chad, sir?"

"They are lying in the bed! Please, someone needs to hurry!"

"Sir, let me talk to the granddaughter, please!"

"Sure. Daisy, they want to speak with you!"

"Hello! Ma'am, everything is going to be okay. I am operator 321 on the line, and I'm going to help you until the hazmat team and paramedics arrive."

"OMG! Please help me. I can't believe my grandparents died!"

"The gentleman on the phone said that your grandparents just got back from China yesterday. Was there anyone else that traveled with them?"

"No! They went alone, just them two," said Daisy, staring straight into Mason's eyes!

"Okay, no problem! Try not to go back into the room. Is there anyone else home with you?"

"No, my big sister is on the way."

"I hear the paramedics. I'm going to hold with you until they arrive. Then you can call your family members. I am sorry to hear what happened to your grandparents."

Daisy started sobbing. "I'm so sorry, Papa and Mama. *Boohhhoohhooh!*"

"The hazmat team has arrived with the paramedics," said Daisy.

"Get over here now, Lilac! Please hurry."

"What's wrong, Daisy? I'm tired. I've been up all night trying to finish this painting. Why are you crying? I can't make out what you're saying… Why do you sound like that?"

"Jack and Jade are unresponsive. They were discovered a few minutes ago. Lilac, please come. I need you!"

Little Daisy Gardenia…

"This agony in my heart is overbearing! What are we going to do now without Jack and Jade? If I could hit the reset button on anything, this would certainly be the time for it. To have it to end this way is a tragedy. Life is so unfair! I regret that we suddenly went out of town when there was no reason to go on a vacation! Unless they all were trying to hide something from me? I would not put it past any of them, including Lilac! She has diversion strategies to a science. I cannot wait to see my sister." *Sniff, sniff.* "She is going to put everything in perspective! My head and heart ache. My first chance at being an adult and it feels like the biggest sham! What would she do? I am going to remain clammed just like Lilac and play this phenomenon.

"Mason, don't open your mouth. Sit tight and keep your mouth shut. Do not spoil this for me. I am sure by now you know to let me handle this with the forensic and hazmat team until Lilac gets here."

"I cannot believe that Jack and Jade are gone."

"What are we going to do about Ava, Theodore, and Sammy, whom we haven't seen in some time now? God knows Jacky is going to bring the heat! I am not talking about guns and talking about something far more dangerous than that! She's coming to take over with a notorious paper trail! "I am so thankful to have Lilac. The Lord designed her especially for me, and she is already a millionaire. Now I see why Jacky said that all we have is each other and to have each other's backs. She has enough room for me. After all, I'm her favorite girl in the world! I am glad we got to say goodbye."

"Excuse me, ma'am. I need to ask you a few questions. We need you to step back a little farther into the driveway because of the hazards waste. COVID-19 has caused death across the nations. I am sorry to see what happened to your grandparents. According to your family chauffer, Mr. and Mrs. Chad went on a three-week vacation to China?"

Daisy spoke slowly, hesitant to answer any questions. "Hi, my name is Daisy. Umm, I didn't go to China with my grandparents. They went alone. Umm, they went on a three-week vacation just to visit the country. Three weeks, I want to say, is the maximum. My grandparents were complaining of body aches, chills, and sweats. They were sick! My grandparents do not normally go to the emergency room for any of their emergency help."

"Daisy, we are familiar with what they call the Wellness Teams that service the Hills of Hollywood," said Detective Summerville. "We are aware of how *they* have their own personal medical team to come and make wellness checks in the privacy of their home. Has anyone come to prescribe any medications to your grandparents?"

"Well, my grandfather, Jack, said he was going to arrange for someone to come and provide aid for him and my grandmother. But no one showed up. I didn't know that they were as sick, or I would've called 911 myself. I had no way of knowing who to contact for them other than my sister, Lilac, who is on the way. I never thought or who would've thought that yesterday was my last day with my grandparents."

"Oh my goodness, news sure travels fast. Who is this pulling up on the driveway?"

"Whoa, it's Ava! Where is she coming from?"

"Ava, Ava, so happy to see you! News sure travels fast around here!"

"Daisy, what is going on? Move out of the way!"

"Jack and Jade died. They believe they died from the coronavirus! They went over to China for at least three weeks or so and returned last night. We all met over Lilac's house! I just do not understand how things happened fast!"

"Why did they have to leave and go to China so abruptly?" said Ava.

"Ava, you need to check yourself seriously… Now is not the time!" said Daisy.

"I need to get a hold of those papers inside that home!"

"Uh, oh my. Now is not the time to think about papers and money! We're talking about the lives of two people that built an empire from scratch! How could you be worried about money and papers? Ava, I cannot believe you!"

"I don't have time for that. Dry up your tears, Daisy. This is reality! This is not the Evan show, okay? We are not going to do this today! Today is the day that I have been sitting back waiting for!" said Ava.

"Do you know what happened to me, my sweet little Daisy? Miss Divine Lovely Child? I will ask you again, do you know what happened to me? Understand that they came for everything I have for helping your sister get ahead in life!"

"What do you mean help my sister get ahead in life? My sister is brilliant!"

"Your sister, brilliant? Brilliant? Brilliant is just to say the least," said Ava. "Ha! Brilliant, ha! Your sister will never be your sister completely, and she don't even know herself. You don't know what you are dealing with. Now move out of the way. Like I said, I need to get into that home and get a hold of these papers!"

"Bitch, please. I cannot wait to see Lilac!"

"Ma'am, who are you?" said Detective Summerville.

"The sole savior of this family and the next loyalist in line! I need to get in there to get the documentation for the beneficiaries from my mom and my dad who died suddenly!"

"You're their oldest daughter?"

"I am their biological daughter, *Ava Chad*, and this is my sweet niece, Daisy, who stayed here with my parents while they died. Oops! Excuse me."

"Get away from me, *clown*! I no longer want you in my presence. I am waiting on my biological sister to arrive Miss Lilac Chad!"

"Well, you wait for your biological sister to get you. I have two or three more biological siblings I must worry about, my sweet Daisy."

"Lilac really needs to hurry up before something strange happens to you, Ava! Like getting your ass kicked across this lawn!"

"Ma'am, I'm going to need you all to step aside! No one will come and pull any documentation out of this house! The size of this house, your grandparents have an executor to this estate! I hope they chose wisely," said Detective Summerville. "Now excuse me while we take care of business here. Thank you!"

"Ava, wait until Lilac gets a hold of this."

"Lilac! Please. Who's Lilac? I taught Lilac everything she knows. If it were not for me, she would have never met Attorney Oats."

"Ah! So it was you that introduced Lilac to Attorney Oats?"

"Yes, it was me that turned Lilac on and off Attorney Oats. Step aside and let this investigation play itself out. I am sure the attorneys will be here soon. Let the games begin. Who we have driving up the runway? Well, if it is not Mr. Theo, or is it Ms. Theo?" said Ava.

"What is going on?" said Theo.

"Duh, you know what is going on. Stand in line, just like me," said Ava. "You know, you never really cared about Jack and Jade! Hell! They never knew you were gay. Did you tell them what you were? Huh? *Ms.* Theo?" said Ava.

"Let me tell you something. You are no different, Miss Motor Booty. Look who's talking. I am sure they left you nothing! Miss Sweet Li'l Ava, who was given everything, what are you mad about? Thought you were on your way to Hollywood. You have done so many horrible things to Jack and Jade. What do you have now? You have nothing," said Theo.

"We'll see who'll have everything in there! As you know, you will be waiting on the sidelines waiting for the investigation to conclude and for their attorneys to arrive, like everyone else. Now please step aside, my sweet little thang," said Ava.

"'Sweet little thang'! Who are you calling your sweet little thang with your negative bank account?! I can guarantee you, ma'am, that they left you absolutely nothing! Do not forget it was you that helped Ms. Lilac *emancipate*. You're jealous of them, and it eats you alive! So you ate a lot of other things along the way, huh, Ava?"

"Ha! Well, we will see about that. What I am going to eat next is filet mignon and lobster for the rest of my life! I am sure there is enough money to go around for generations to come! Ha! Welp, let's just see," said Ava.

"What is taking Lilac so long? Where is she? I need her. Where are you, where are you, where are you?" said Daisy. "I need you."

"Oh, Ms. Lilac! She does not drive anymore, huh. Jumping out of her fancy Porsche. Oh, she has Ms. Wafiya with her. Grand ole Ms. Wafiya that sticks around and has a guesthouse in the back of Lilac's home. Fuckin' immigrant! So where are you going to go, Daisy? Ms. Wafiya has a guesthouse in the back?"

"My sister and I will have everything! Lilac! I am so happy to see you! Lilac!"

"What is going on here?" said Lilac. "Daisy, Daisy, Daisy, I love you so much. Please do not cry. What is going on here?" said Lilac. "Ava, Theo, I'm so glad to see you on this sad occasion! I am going in there. Let met in! Let me go, let me go," said Lilac.

"Ma'am, step aside! You cannot come inside! Your parents have been to China. There is a disease that has spread across the nation," said Detective Summerville. "Thousands have died in China, ma'am! We believe your grandparents were victims of the coronavirus that is spreading vastly."

"Oh they came over my house last night and were not feeling too well! We laughed, we joked, we cried, we ate, and we hugged! They said they did not feel good! Oh my god, I had no idea they were this sick! Oh my god, I had no idea they were this sick! I feel so bad. I feel so bad! I need to get in just one more time to hold them. Just one more time! Please, my sweet Jack. What will I do now? What are we going to do? Oh my god!"

"Oh my god, Lilac. You, ma'am, are well off than all of us! No one is standing as high as you, Miss Emancipated Lily. How did you know to get ahead of everyone else? Can you share the secret, Lilac? I need a secret too! Stop all the crying because I am sure you know your mom is the oldest! The battle is on! You think you are something? You have not seen anything from your mother! You want to know more? I have been down in the gutter and come back up! I gained the same exact strength as your mother," said Ava.

"Aye, Lilac, did your momma tell you about your daddy... Steven?" Ava continued. "I will break you down, standing right here at this death scene Lilac!"

"You know nothing about him!" shouted Lilac. "What is wrong with you, Ava? What has gotten into you? Why are you acting like this? You are someone that I looked up to! You were like everything to me! Why? What have I have done to you to make you treat me as such?"

"Well, let me count the ways. From the start, you are prettier than I am. You won my mother and my father's hearts from the start. Let me see, you done the exact same thing your mother did and broke my father's heart when she suddenly packed up and moved to Washington DC! I was his favorite child with nothing to worry about! With Jacky living on the other side of the world, everything belonged to me."

"Daisy and I have done nothing to you, bitter bitch! Jack and Jade has died, and we will never be able to see them again. Everything is not about money, Ava! Money is not everything! I have my own money. I have my own skill. I have my own ambitions and drive, and I will make it!" said Lilac.

"You said it correctly, Miss Emancipated Lily. Taking care of herself since I was fifteen years old! Taking care of my sister since the day she was conceived. She never has *anything* to worry about. She does not need anything from you! We do not need anything from none of you! In fact, Daisy, you do not need anything in that house. Everything is contaminated!"

"Aye, Lilac, your mouth is contaminated!" said Ava.

"Let us not talk about anyone's mouth, Miss Nasty Ava! We are not going to talk about anyone's mouth after you recently picked up an award for 'Best Exotic Mouth of the Year'!" Theo said, snapping his fingers. "Yes, we are not going to talk about contamination!" said Theo.

"Here comes the attorney," said Lilac.

"Hello there, Lilac, Daisy, Theo, and my sweet Ava," said Attorney Akyol. "Theo, hello, son!"

"How are you? We are not going to act like we do not know each other are we, Akyol?"

"Theo, now is not the time. Your parents just died!"

Everyone was looking to be in shock that Theo and Mr. Akyol had an affair.

"Attorney Anderson sent me to inform everyone of a meeting in the morning to talk about this. She has a ten-o'clock opening at the office. She can talk then. Jack and Jade came by the office a few months ago to make some revisions to their estate. Some recent events took place, and they made a lot of revisions in the will and testament."

"I wonder what kind of revisions could have been made," said Ava.

"We are not going to discuss that right now. I came by to see if there was anything I could do to help my grandparents," said Lilac.

"Since I'm the executor of the estate at this moment, my sister Jacky is living in Washington DC at an unknown address. I doubt if you will be able to contact her. To add, she gave up her children for adoption to my parents. She will want nothing to do with this," said Ava.

"Wait a minute there, Ms. Ava! I am the attorney advisor! I am going to repeat who I am to Mr. and Mrs. Jack and Jade Chad. I am the attorney advisor that assists to represent them and their estate, so this means I am everything to them! This also means I know what is going on! I have written documents for everything! So we are not going to talk about who I am! I am here to let you know what I can do for you! So if you do not like that, Ava, then my suggestion for you is to find something else to do until it is your turn," said Attorney Akyol.

"My turn to finish flatlining that ass said, Theo."

"Has Ava been in haste like this toward all of you?"

"She has been acting this way towards all of us," said Lilac, Daisy, and Theo.

"I will take care of you," said Attorney Akyol. "I am going to head back to the office and see you tomorrow in the morning at ten o'clock sharp!"

"I cannot believe this!" said Ava.

"Ma'am, we are going to go ahead and move those bodies to the mortuary. I am going to need someone to come and identify the bodies of your grandparents in the mortuary."

"Oh my god, I cannot believe I am hearing someone say that someone needs to identify Jack and Jade! This got to be the saddest day of our lives," said Lilac!

Lemon Citrus Charm...

"Ah, I cannot believe we are going to do this." Ava pretended to dry her eyes. "Enough of the tearjerker! You are so fake. You heard when Attorney Akyol said that the will and testament was changed just a few months prior!" said Ava.

"I do not think anything else more can hurt me, Lilac! When I helped you sell your first painting, you never thought about me! You only were my friend that pretended to love me so much, and I bought into your game. Trusted you so much I was able to put you in contact with Oaks! Then when you became old enough, you started dating his son Mansy! You have your whole life planned out in front of you, Lilac! You are a celebrity artist. Yes, you are so everything that Jack wanted me to be! *You took it all!* They had nothing out of me and my sister Jackie, so he gave it all to you, and if that is so, I will battle you in court until it is all over with! You met your maker!"

"Ava, we are not going to do this right now. I am going to take the high road on this one! I will meet you at the top 'cause I would not drop to the gutter to meet you! I'm taking my sister, and we are going to go. You and Theo can figure this out because Daisy and I have a meeting with Attorney Anderson at ten o'clock in the morning. I suggest you freshen up, dear. Grease them elbows! I have the drive and ambition that you always wished you had! Ava, you talked about the ambition that my mother has. It is not a fraction of what was living inside of me! I am Lilac, honey. I am strong, beautiful, trendsetter Lilac, who paints the town the way I want it to look! Do not forget that!"

Ava stood in silence looking as if she could take Lilac and Daisy's life right now!

You would never be half the woman my sister is. You would never be able to meet our standards. We were not raised to be like you. We were not given everything! I'm able to respect life and give love,

84

and I will fuck you up at the same time! Don't forget, Big Lilac and Li'l Daisy were born in Washington, DC, Uhland Terrace Northeast. *Pooh.* Something that you were not able to do because you were given everything from the beginning. Maybe if the shoe were on the other foot, you would have learned how to appreciate your parents much more. Now my advice to you is, back away from my sweet Lilac because she is not going to fight you. It is going to be me!"

"You're a quiet storm!" said Mason.

"Daisy, I've never seen this side of you before," said Theo. "I never knew you had this *fire* inside of you! I like the new Daisy. I love it! You need to keep her of out more often. Her mouth is equivalent to Ava when it comes to attitude! Except nobody is trashier than Ava! I am so glad to know that, at least. Yes, I am gay and I turned this town up and slept with every rich old man out there! In addition to that, I have a P-H-A-T bank account! Incorporating my own condominium! What do you have, Ava? Nothing! Still sitting around waiting on Jack and Jade. So you sat and you waited until they died. You may be left out in the dust, ma'am! So long, I'm going home! You can sit here at this crime scene by yourself."

"Mr. Mason? I did not know you are still here. You were sitting over there in your limousine. Aww, Mr. Mason, it has been so nice to have you around, and it has been an amazing ride, but your services are no longer needed here. What are you sticking around for?" said Ava.

"Child, watch your filthy mouth. That was my brother and my sister, my friends! I have been working with them for more than thirty years! I will sit here until all is said and over! I watched you grow up and blossom into a beautiful woman. The lifestyle you are living was a great embarrassment! Triple X screen for the world to see! *Porno!* You belittle them after all the arduous work they done! They have done so much in their lifetime! I am going to pray for you! I will sit! I have the right to see them off. This was my job, to sit here and take orders! Yes, orders from my friend, my brother! So I know one thing—you are not going to sit out here and wait for documents! There are no documents in the house! You should know, I take Daddy everywhere, and Daddy does not have a document inside that house! Now Akyol came here a little while ago, and he said you guys should meet at ten o'clock in the morning. I suggest you get ready to do that."

"Mister Mason, you do not know me well. You do not know me that well. You stay tuned for the next episode because it is coming your way and everybody else's way! I got enough channels to feed the universe! I would not let Lilac own everything, and I have nothing! Mister Mason, you run and tell that!"

"This is a *home*. It was always a house to you. Therefore, you were told to leave it! You are the only one out of everyone that has no house, no home. I will call you when they are on their way to the coroners' office."

"I will be on my way. Okay, Mister Mason."

"Do that!"

CHAPTER 14

Snap Dragon

"Good morning, everyone!"

"Hello, Ms. Anderson. I'm glad to see you all around. Prompt, ten o'clock, on time. So let's get straight to business. Have a seat. I am holding the latest will and testament from Jack and Jade. They came February 24, 2020, to make some revisions. I also know that none of you knew Jack and Jade hit the lottery in Washington DC. They paid to keep their names out of the eyes of the public. They did not want you or everyone else to know about the fortune that they had run into to add onto the fortune that they have already accumulated during the years of them working so hard to build their empire! They put the A in Architect, furniture that lasts forever.

"Sit back and relax. There will be some turbulence along the way. I am going to read this declaration of facts that is sworn and written to be true, so help me God. After I am done, I will have my assistant make everyone copies."

The Last Will and Testament
Jack Chad and Jade Chad

Pursuant to the California Probate Code

We, Jack Chad and Jade Chad, residents of
the state of California. Being of sound mind, not
acting under duress or undue influence, in any
understanding the nature and extent of all my
property and of this deposition, we do hereby
make, publish, and declare this document to be
our last will and testament.

Hereby revoke any and all other wills
beforehand.

I direct all sales, debt, and expenses of our
last and final goodbye, funeral, and burial to be
paid soon after our death. We hereby authorize
Lilac Chad to settle and discharge our debt. Lilac
Chad is appointed absolute discretion on any
claims made against our estate.

I nominate Lilac Chad in the state of
California to serve as our representative in
our position of property. If both real and personal, whatever suited Lilac Chad, our primary
beneficiary.

Daisy Chad is the second beneficiary if Lilac
Chad cannot pursue this bequest.

There will be *no third beneficiary*. Daisy
Chad will take the entire estate, including any
capital.

If Lilac Chad and Daisy Chad cannot take
on this responsibility, then any of our property
can be readily distributed and donated to any
domestic violence organization.

Jack Chad and Jade Chad request that any
personal property cannot be donated if Lilac

Chad and Daisy Chad cannot stand for this will and testament.

If ANYONE that is not mentioned in the last will and testament tries to contest or attack this will and testament, under the State of California, this will and testament will not be revoked and shall not be disposed. Jack Chad, The Man.

"Now, family, I need you to adjust yourself by what you just heard. Does anyone care for a drink? Perhaps a glass of water? Wine?"

"No, thank you. I'm ready to get out of the dry-ass meeting. It is not a shock factor! I knew she would get everything!" said Ava.

"Jackie, do you have things you would like to say?" said Anderson.

"It sure feels good to see my girls!"

Lilac, Daisy, Ava, Theo, and Sammy did not pay attention to the monitor facing them on the wall. They were confounded with surprise!

"I cannot believe you are giving us a virtual visit as if you are in prison! Jack and Jade knew you best! It would have been nice to see you in person, Jackie! You have a lot of nerve!" said Lilac.

"See, Lilac? What did I tell you? You cannot trust her! Do not let her back in your heart, Lilac!"

"Daisy, you know darn well I will not shame my mother! It is nice to see you, virtual woman," said Lilac.

"Daisy, you both look beautiful as usual. I never thought that my parents would have left me anything since we did not get along. I have no regrets," said Jacky.

"You have no regrets? WTF! After you gave Lilac and me up for adoption without notice BITCH! You threw us on an airplane alone! You tricked us! We arrived in California and have not laid eyes on you since! Lilac and I were thinking when were we going to see you again in the flesh. A Bissshh show up on Virtual Love and Hugs, said Daisy.

"What is this? You are as cold as ice," said Lilac. "I see exactly why Jade adopted us. We never stood a chance with you!"

"I see you are doing rather good for yourself. You taking diligent care of your sister. What are you complaining about? I do not see what the big deal is. *You* have all the millions," said Jackie. "Excuse me, Ms. Anderson. Since I am part of this exclusive meeting, can you please expose how much money my sweet daughter Lilac inherited?"

"Before you two get into an intense argument, I would like to have a family discussion with you! Are you finished?"

"Yes, we are."

"Lilac, you have inherited seven hundred million dollars," said Attorney Anderson.

"Oh my god! I did not think that Jack and Jade were so well off! What am I going to do with so much money?"

"Not so fast, Lilac. Jack and Jade worked extremely hard to build this dynasty. I am going to continue to represent you as a long-term family attorney. Lilac and Daisy, recognize that you have family in me.

"I need all of you to give it some consideration to maybe help each other out. Give a little space because you may need these same family members to serve you in the future."

"He gives me the creeps! Him and his girlfriend," said Lilac. "You look at me so strange? Is it something about me, or there is something about you? Whatever it is, my hair stands up on the back of my neck!"

Everyone turned over and looked at Sammy and his new girlfriend.

"I come in peace for the sake of my father and my mother."

"Come on now, Sammy. You know you have no business here! It is a wonder that Jack did not mention that in his will," said Attorney Anderson.

"What is going on there? Did I miss something?" said Jackie.

"How are you going to find out what is going on? You did not even take the time to get on a plane to and fly across the country to see about your children that you have not seen in *five long years*," said Ava.

"Jacky, you cannot reclaim your time on this one. I am the one that holds the power! The keys to the realm! Everyone will get a piece of the pie," said Lilac. "I will not be like you, Jackie. I would never have the heart you have. None of you will get what you think you deserve. However, I will make sure all of you walk away today with a two-million-dollar check! Excluding this guy here that makes the hair stand up on the back of my neck! I am not giving you anything. Jack and Jade gave you nothing."

"No one can blame you for not giving him anything, Lilac," said Theo.

"We will not drag this out any longer. I will cut you all checks. Pass your identification to my paralegal and help yourselves to anything you like while waiting. My paralegal will get back with you in a moment. All please sit in the waiting area. Lilac and Daisy, I need to talk to you."

"Yes, Ms. Anderson."

"Jackie, this meeting is over. Please contact the front office and provide your account information to receive the wire transfer."

"Yes, I will send her the same two million dollars. The only person that I will not send anything to the so-called priest. He is a creep!"

"Okay, Lilac, this meeting is over with Jackie."

"Thank you, my dear daughter. Thank you for loving me."

"Thank you for bringing me into this world and making the perfect mistake by giving me up." Lilac ended this conversation with her. "Goodbye, Jacky."

"Lilac, you have a lot of money in your pocket. You are also exceptionally talented, young lady. There is no need for you to pull money out of any account at this moment. As a certified tax accountant, my advice to you is to save and invest. I will help you to invest. Jack left his money with you, a young woman, to run his empire. He has a lot of faith in you and Daisy. I am here for you. I am going to arrange for you to meet my business partner, Tank. We call him Tank for short because he is from another country and has four names. He will tell you his real name. Here is his number. Give him a call in the morning. You will need someone to protect you. I will also call Mr. Mason and get him on your team."

"Thank you, Ms. Anderson. Thank you for being in my corner. Daisy and I need you and your guidance and support. I'm sure it will take us a long way."

"Jack and Jade were my friends. I'm going to make sure you are fine! You will be the first billionaire by the age of twenty-two!"

"Ms. Anderson, thank you."

"Come on, Lilac. Wafiya is outside waiting on us."

"Ava, you are still my favorite girl! Please take the money and invest in something. Show me what you got! Theo, I already know what you are capable of. Do it for yourself and please stay connected. Let us clean up our acts and continue to build this empire."

CHAPTER 15

Teleflora Divine Peace

LILAC TIPTOED THROUGH HER HOME and out the back door she went, dressed in the one-piece body leopard suit and purple wig and purple metallic claws on each fingertip.

Tonight, the moon is at its fullest. I'm going to play this game to the very end. This leopard cat bodysuit fits superb! I am going trick-or-treating tonight to give that priest a blessing of a lifetime. He won't even see it coming, not even in the darkest of night! I wish these metal claws had venom in them; that would make it even better. This black cat maintained her role long enough. The dreams I've encountered are real! He will pay tonight for taking my innocence. When Jack and Jade cross over, they will see the priest pass them by! He's doomed, this one I'll take care of myself!

Lilac, with the steel cat claws clutching the steering wheel, sped down the boulevard with the ugly cry on her beautiful face, tears.

I'm going to cut this motherfucker's eyes out with my bare hands! This death scene will be one that no one could ever imagine!

This is a great parking spot, alongside this wooded area. This must me my lucky night; the streetlights are broken. When I'm done with Sammy, neither Ava nor Theo will be able to identify his face. He'll stay in the morgue and be buried in an unmarked grave. I want California to implement this scene in a movie. It will be gruesome and untimely, that's a fact.

Sammy was walking down the street, betting on taking another young girl's innocence as he sang and walked along the dark wooded area. "Jesus is my friend, Jesus you are... I'm looking for that special one tonight... These fools abide by a man no one has ever seen!"

Lilac eased from behind the black Porsche and stared, walking behind Sammy.

"Who are you? A black cat in the night? Hey, baby. What's your name?"

"Kitty Kitty in the city!"

"Here, Kitty Kitty. Come here. I got a big ball of yarn you can play with if you let me stroke your back and pull your tail."

"Sure, you can..."

Sammy turned around and began to walk towards the black cat. Lilac began to strut like a whore towards Sammy, holding a gun close to her hip and one hand free!

"Meow!" she said as she raised her right hand, dug deep into his face with metal cat claws, and pistol-whipped Sammy with the gun!

"Ouuuchhhh!" Sammy tried to run, but Lilac had the gun to his throat.

"Walk your ass through this path, you nasty piece of shit! You don't even know who I am!"

"Please, lady, I don't know you? Please don't kill me!"

"You already killed me when I was ten years old! This is Lilac, you rapist! Tonight will be your last night walking the streets. No more taking advantage of people!"

"Lilac, what did I do to you! Ooowww. Please don't scratch my face again with those metal claws!"

"We are deep enough in these woods now, bastard! Take you clothes off!"

"What? Ouuuchhhh! Please, Lilac, I'm sorry for what I did to you. I was wrong! Please don't kill me! Ouuchhhhh!"

Bloop, Bloop!

"No more noise from you." She began to inject Sammy's dead body with embalming fluid, mummifying his body to slow the bleeding.

Lilac began to saw Sammy limbs off his body, scratching his face until it was unrecognizable. She got in her car and drove off, scattering the body parts as she drove down the boulevard in the darkness.

That was a joy, taking his life!

Two days later...

The funeral was beautiful. Everyone was wearing lavender to match Jack and Jade—lavender and white.

"I believe Jack and Jade are smiling from the heavens, Lilac."

"I am expecting company in a little while, Daisy."

"Who is coming over?"

"A doctor that owns the hospital."

"Yaasss. My dear sister, you sure know how to pick them!"

"Yes, I do, sister. I am so glad to have you as my sister to tell me the truth about life."

"Always use your body last, Daisy. Never be anxious to jump in the bed with anyone! Since you want to do modeling, we are going to line that model gig up for you."

"Lilac, I'm ready to be on my own..."

"Have you lost your mind, Daisy? The difference... I can take care of myself. You cannot take care of yourself. That is your barrier. Your money was put into a trust fund, Daisy. *Copacetic*, that is the word of the day!"

"Okay, Lilac, I will not move in haste. I will let you guide me through the maze. Lilac, my heart is not designed like yours. I'm not giving Mother any of me or my fortune, and that includes Father. They left for a reason, and it broke Jack and Jade's hearts. The trust fund is an advantage point for me. Look at Ava, God knows she needs something! Ha ha ha," said Daisy.

"Let the church say amen to what you said, Daisy! What happened to Ava was a shame. Don't let that happen to you, Li'l Daisy.

She should have tried to be more of herself than like Jacky" said Daisy. "Look am "hangry" right now," said Daisy.

Lily at the breakfast table...

Lilac gazed out the windows, watching the lavender daisy garden as the sun beamed through the trees, not giving one thought of the monstrous crime that she committed.

"Lilac, did you see the news? Dead body parts were scattered across the boulevard. No one can identify the body... They have to perform a DNA analysis to identify the body."

"I couldn't care less whose body that was. I have a hot date tonight, Wafiya. Wait until you get a load of this tea! Wafiya, the doctor that cared for me that night reached out to me. He was interested in taking me out on a date. What do you think about that, Wafiya?"

"I mean there isn't so much that I can tell you. Guide your own path. You always have been that way. I think you know what's best for you. How old is he? Are you talking about the older man?"

"Wafiya, I am not really looking at the age. I'm looking at the quality of the person in how he treats me. How he makes me feel. The way he looks into my eyes. That night, things were gruesome. He looked past the trauma to my face. Somehow he still saw the beauty through all the purple, blue, and black bruises. That night was the night he saw the beauty. I never thought I would see myself again."

"Well, that explains a lot. He's been sending you flowers?"

"Yes, he has, Wafiya. I hope this will bring joy and warmth into my world. I certainly can use a break from trauma. I didn't ask to come in this world, but I'm sure glad to be in it!

"Wafiya, have you seen my masterpiece? Did you see the embedded veil and the red lipstick on the black-and-white painting of myself? Only the closest to me know it's me! I love a mystery. Just think whatever it auctions for triples in years to come."

"Someone has been calling you from Sotheby's to auction it off!"

"That was the plan—to go auction it off—but since the loss of Jack and Jade, everything had to be redirected for another time."

"I can understand."

"I thank you, Wafiya, for cooking breakfast for Daisy and me."

"I appreciate you, Lilac."

CHAPTER 16

Peruvian Lily

"I'M SO GLAD YOU WERE able to come over and see me!"

"Lilac, it's been quite some time since I last saw your beautiful face," said Adnan. "I'm so happy that you gave me the opportunity to be in your life."

"I would have it no other way. I mean, what do you do with a person that sends fresh flowers every week for five years and without a kiss or touch? I can't tell you how grateful I am to have you in my life. Although, I thought it would play out...whole time you never dropped the ball."

"I would never drop the ball. I love you too much."

"How can you love me? We've never been out to eat, shopping, or anything else. How do you know I'm the one you love so much? Have you ever thought about the age difference between you and me?"

"I haven't thought much about the age difference, but what I can say is, I thought about you. All I can think of is you, Lilac."

"Thank you. I thought about you, Adnan, in the fondest way. You entered my life when I needed someone the most, and I can't wait to get you in my big beautiful bed."

"Look at what you done to me, trigger wrapped around my leg hearing your voice. I can't go another second without being inside of you and dive into your waterfall. Lead the way... My tongue will touch every hole in your body today, Ms. Lilac."

"Follow me, Adnan. Please let me help you fulfill your desires."

Lilac led the way to the palace-style bedroom she prepared for this day, the smell of rosemary, silk lavender sheets, and lilac flower petals leading to her bed.

"Lilac, your mouth and tongue wrapped around my rod feels like heaven. Please don't make me cum too fast. I want this to last forever..."

Lilac kissed Adnan passionately until she reached his lips.

"Oh yeah, that's what you been thinking about for five years? Let me show you what I've been thinking. The doctor is in your house. My sweet Lilac, baby, your skin smells like flowers seep from your sweat. Your beautiful round breasts, I love your pretty light-skinned nipples. And your pussy tastes so good and so wet! Thank you, baby, for saving it for me..."

"Adnan, this is going to be a long night. I hope your phone is off..."

"What phone, baby? I called you from my car phone."

"Adnan, please dont stop. Beat this kitty kat up, apply more pressure please." They began to make passionate love like a marathon.

The next morning

"Adnan, you took me for a ride last night. It feels good to wake up beside you, handsome."

"Lilac, I want to marry you. I can't wait to give you children with your eyes."

"Marry me and children? Adnan, you are scaring me! You are talking children after the first night."

"You're not just talking to anybody, Lilac. I'm in the billionaire club!"

"You are speaking to a billionaire artist. Speaking of billionaire, the painting I created during the time of Jack and Jade's death, it auctioned for $25,000,000. An anonymous buyer bought it. Would that anonymous buyer happen to be you?"

"It wouldn't be anonymous if I told you who bought it, right?"

"Just hold me and kiss me. Give me all of you, Adnan. Love me any way you know best. Mold me into the woman you want me to be."

"Lilac, that's a strong statement. I want you to remain the strong young entrepreneur you are. I fell in love with your mind first. That is what I love the most."

"I'm so turned on and intrigued by you. I can't wait to see what waits in the future for us!"

"I have to jet out of here to the hospital. I have sick people waiting on me, Lilac."

"Okay, Adnan...I have a flight to catch to New York. I'm auctioning another painting I've been holding on to since I lost my sweet grandparents."

"Love you, Lilac. Call me when your flight lands."

"Adnan, next time I see you, we're going to play with some edible body paint..."

"I'm looking forward to learning how to paint!"

*****

"In the event that I decide to go with that weaner, I'm going to have to put up quite a performance for the rest of my life. These are the only things that keep this impoverished youngster alive, his physical appearance, his physical body, and his character as well as his money. His best bet is to hold on to each and every one of them. However, he understands how to make use of all he has on his bed... and it works for hours at a time! The honey on the tip of your tongue works like a rose in that it touches everything in the vaginal area, including the uterus, fallopian tubes, and ovary! Because of his masculine bulk pressing up against mine, not to mention that wicked mouthpiece of his, my vaginal walls were strained to their breaking point, Daisy."

"Regardless of your feelings about his man part, it certainly puts a smile on your face, looking at you Lilac! Everything about this experience has been wonderful! Remember that you are still desirable just like any other woman, and never lose sight of that!"

"Daisy, I've made the decision to cancel my planned trip out of town for today. I'd prefer to accept Adnan's invitation to visit him in Paris and accompany him to Africa. He communicated in my language…a language that is rich in vocabulary. When it comes to money conversations, there is a specific technique to use, and there are seven stages to follow to be successful! I'm grateful that we've always had that in common when it comes to picking the right team for the job."

"I will notify you tiny sister of my departure for Paris as soon as I receive confirmation from him via text message. The exact date will be announced later, so stay tuned."

"That was fast… He didn't waste any time in responding and informing me that he had already booked my flight. As you can see, he recognizes me, Li'l Suga!"

"He does, in fact. When your private plane lands, take a video for me! I am overjoyed for you, Lilac, because things are finally going your way."

"I will notify you, tiny sister, when I land in Paris!"

"*Bonjour*, Lilac!"

"He mentioned one thing in particular. According to his message, I don't have to do any packing. Thank goodness, because between making sure your suitcase doesn't weigh more than fifty pounds and making it to the departure gate before the doors close, flying can be a stressful experience."

"When it comes to all the changes in airports as a result of the coronavirus pandemic, money is king, and you can ignore airline guidelines and policies if you have that bag, my dear," said Lilac.

"Prepare yourself, Mason. I have to get to the airport in order to catch my flight to Paris!"

It appeared that someone in Paris was completely swept off their feet last night!

The city of love

"Hello, my darling. How are you today? I'm relieved to see that your feet have finally landed on solid ground. My darling, arrangements have been made for you to be able to participate in all the excursions that you desire. The hypnotic effect of your eyes has me mesmerized, Lilac…"

Once Adnan made his way up to the young emancipated Lily and kissed her from her toes on up, he moved on to Lilac's bald vagina, which he gently eased his way up to from the bottom of her miniskirt. Lilac pressed upon against the tip of his pointed tongue, her mini skirt completely obscuring his face. With Lilac's sweet love filling his heart, Adnan couldn't help but succumb to his temptation. Adnan had completely forgotten about his reservations by the time he had finished cleaning Lilac up and stroking her. Lilac had to take time to recover from the sexual healing Adnan demonstrated.

*****

"I finally realized that all the luxury Birkin bags were inspired by the flavors and are arranged on the couch! I'm a Lucky girl!"

There wasn't enough art in Paris to fill Lilac's day with visits to see Monet, Picasso, and Degas. She was in fashion nirvana with each piece of clothing she donned from a different designer. In the heart of Europe's most vibrant city, it is impossible to miss the city's culinary and artistic offering on every corner, said Lilac. From cruising the Canal Saint-Martin and baking the best croissants to us grinding in the city's most elaborate cabaret clubs. Remember us stumbling across the street art we was "Lit". Adnan this is an experience "the girl" will never forget. Sealing this with a kiss babes, said Lilac.

"This week went by so fast in France's capital, Paris, one of my favorite cities on the planet. It doesn't matter where I go. When I travel to the well-known capital, the city of love, I always have a unique experience just as if I were traveling anywhere else. In addition to being beautiful, Paris is a wonderful place for a romantic getaway, Lilac. When I look at your beautiful face, I am filled with joy there are so many scenic views you have yet to discover in your artistic world and I want to be that Man to capture your every essence through these lens."

"Adnan, you've already won my heart with your stay at the Londoner and the Parisian charm you've displayed."

"Despite the fact that Paris is regarded as Europe's most starry-eyed metropolis, you are the star that shines the brightest in my heart. Everything I would do for you, Lilac."

"Going to Clos Maggiore for dinner, doing some shopping in Seven Dials, swimming in Hampstead Heath, and taking a walk through one of the several monarch's parks are all things. Adnan you made sure that I reached my pinnacle while in Paris. All the cuddling and kissing we've been doing is going to cost you a child, Adnan!"

"All I want really is for you to have my baby. The next flight is to Africa for my queen," said Adnan!

*****

"Because of the natural wonders of Africa, Adnan, I have become more closely connected than you could ever imagine. After a traumatic event occurred in my life, in an instant, my family made the decision to remain silent. Exploring the continent has been a truly enlightening experience for me… They would make the decision to go on these extravagant trips while I would be left behind to recover from my wounds. There was absolutely no ill will between them and me, I'm certain. After all, it appears to me that it was the only way they knew how to deal with such a tragic event. To you, my suga zaddy, whether it's a private plunge pool, a view of the Serengeti, or even your very own remote island, you've made it a point to blow the minds of the ladies who come here. You're the current hot topic on my mind!" exclaimed Lilac.

"Since the first time I laid eyes on you, you've been my possession. When it comes to adventure and change, Africa has something to offer you. The motherland is the perfect place. Looking at all the beautiful shades of brown, looking like a chocolate rainbow. There adventures are on the table, from hiking to the summit of

Mount Kilimanjaro to sleeping under the stars in Zambia! Our position as king and queen in Africa is undisputed, and I have the financial means to protect you and your family," said Adnan. Love is in the air because of the expression on your face. It's the perfect recipe for chemistry. I've watched Africa heal you, young lady, and you've enjoyed the island's private pleasures while I've stood by and watched…"

"Your assistance in creating a bucket list for my time in Africa has been invaluable, and I am leaving feeling refreshed and rejuvenated. Thank you so much for all your assistance."

"This has been a beautiful three months journey, my love, and it must come to an end. I'm well aware that the entire world is on the lookout for me right now."

"It's been beautiful, and I have a new strength. I'm going to miss the glamping safaris the most," said Lilac. "I love you, Adnan."

CHAPTER 17

Aristolochia

"Twenty-five, twenty-five, thirty. Thirty-five, thirty-five, forty. Do I have forty over here? Fifty, fifty-five, sixty, sixty-five hundred. Can I get seventy thousand? Ninety to the man in the pinstriped suit. Can I get one hundred thousand? One hundred and six thousand over here. Can I get one hundred and twenty thousand? Three hundred and fifty thousand to the lady in the purple dress. Four hundred and fifty thousand. Do I have five hundred thousand to the lady standing over there with the silver dress on? Can I get six hundred twenty five thousand? Going once, going twice. Sold to the gentleman standing again in the back with the black suit. Another painting sold by one of our famous and favorite artist, Lilac Chad of Santa Barbara, California. Gentleman standing at the back, please go and give your information to our representatives in the back. Everyone please step aside. This concludes our auction in New York Plaza."

"Oh god, Lilac."

"Yes, Adnan?"

"You are simply amazing. What would I do without you?"

"What would we do without each other? I am so happy that we are gifts to each others lives," said Adnan.

"Lilac, you make more money than I do. Even though I am the CEO of a hospital, mostly all my money is divided and put into trust funds, and you are excellent at planning."

"Thank you for recognizing my professional attributes as an artist. That means a lot. You are paying attention."

"Isn't that something? I'm so glad that you and I have so many sunny days. I cannot believe you are carrying our baby."

"Our new baby girl," said Lilac.

"Lilac, I know painting is truly your first love. However, I'm going to need you to take a step back from painting. At least until the baby is born."

"Yes, I know, but for some reason, I love inhaling all the greatness of it."

"Lilac, I plan for us to go away and take a trip."

"Take a trip where? Where would you like to go?"

"I would like to stay in Hawaii. It's nice and warm. The people on the island are just so beautiful, nice, great food, water, and rest and relaxation. You would love it there," said Adnan.

"I think so too. The warmth of the island. Where would we stay there? It never ran across my mind to buy a home in Hawaii. I never thought I would be going there."

"Don't worry about that, I got you," said Adnan. "Lilac, when are we going to marry? Am I good enough for you? Do I make enough money for you to marry me?"

"I am not thinking about marriage right now. My mind and heart are focused on delivering a healthy, beautiful, and happy baby girl. Marriage is so far from my mind."

"All the tea in China couldn't stop me from being with you right now, Lilac."

"You know, all the tea in China right now probably isn't any good. so please do not bring me any tea right now."

"But, Lilac, you are all that I need."

"You are all that I need, Adnan. Let's just go and enjoy the night here in New York. You have bought me that huge property in Bel Air, I think it's safe to say even though we are not married, I would like for us to sign a prenup. It's not that I don't love you, Adnan. It's for protection. The law in California varies on domestic relationships."

"I understand perfectly that it is for protection. I'm looking at it the same way you are."

"I've learned to think of feelings last, Adnan. I want to protect what's given to me. I have just as much money as you do, if not more! I am my own woman and a self-made one at her best! You cannot take that away from me."

"Never would I ever try to take anything away from you, Lilac. I never thought of that. I thought we were going to be building each other. Lilac, sometimes the way you act and talk makes me think that you have no intention of marrying me."

"I never said I did not want to marry you. All I said is, I'm not ready for marriage. I am still young, Adnan."

"Even though you are young, I still know what I want."

"Well, I know what I want too. Can we not talk about marriage? You are making us nauseous."

"Okay, Lilac, we won't talk about marriage until after Lily breathes more beauty into this relationship. Would you like to go somewhere to get something good to eat?"

"Adnan, let's just enjoy the moment while we are in our hotel room off Fifth Avenue, New York City. It's so beautiful at night—the glitz, glamour, and the bright lights. A little shopping wouldn't hurt. I want to go to the Chanel shop and get a personalized handbag to take back home. Adnan, have you ever noticed how people stare at you? You light up the room with your beautiful smile and your pearly white teeth, and your dark skin—all that melanin is so beautiful."

"Lilac, I've charmed plenty of women right out their panties. Black, Hispanic, Caucasian, Brazilian, and Asian, you name it. I have had them all."

"Just because the cat looks good doesn't mean the kitty can be tamed. I'm noticeably confident as well, Adnan. My grandparents and mother brought us up in the long-standing tradition where the lighter you are, the better off your life will be. No pun intended to hurt you…"

"Your grandparents have it wrong. I bet they never thought you would be here with me. A young Black CEO of his own hospital, how about that? Black with pearly white teeth, eight pack, and more than eight inches that you cannot keep your pretty lips off, Lilac."

"Wow! Just go ahead and tell the world, Adnan, what I cannot keep my mouth off. That goes both ways, handsome."

"I'm not complaining about it, Lilac."

"Remember how your entire mouth fit gently over my vah-jay. How about that? Sucking the babies yeast outta me."

They both began to laugh!

"So are we going out to eat? Do you want to go out and buy Chanel bag? Whatever your heart desires, Lilac."

"I will pass right now, Adnan. Sitting back in this plush reclining chair, thinking how I just reached one billion in cash. This does not include liquid assets. I am the first Black billionaire in the family. Let us ensure we get that prenup together as soon as possible. I am going to arrange a date as soon as I get back to California. We have our family meetings once a month, anyway, and surprisingly, everyone is doing well. I need to get plenty of rest. I got a flight to catch tomorrow to meet with Kay. I have not seen and put my eyes on Theo. Must meet with Ava. Daisy is doing fabulous in her modeling career," said Lilac.

"This bed feels way too good. Do you mind taking my shoes off? I'm beat."

"I notice your attitude has adjusted since I have gotten pregnant. You are not even around as much."

"Do you think you are ready for this baby?"

"Lilac, why would you say such a thing? I'm always ready for you!"

"I think I have done a lot for us not to be married and all. Donating one of my paintings to the hospital for the Neo Ward signed by *the* Lilac Chad. It does not get any better than that, Adnan. Sometimes we put ourselves in positions to help others for them to quickly forget what happened."

"I won't, Lilac."

"This foot massage feels divine. Massaging my hands, Adnan, what you trying to do? This makes me feel some type of good in the bed, and your big hands on my belly… Lily is moving around, Adnan. You feel that?"

"I got to go the bathroom," said Adnan.

"Adnan, I noticed whenever we are beginning to get in the mood, you go in the bathroom. Are you on sexual stimulation medication?"

"No! I do not need that to get up!"

"I must ask. After all, you are a doctor that has access to all types of medications. Lately, you have a split personality. From what I've seen, you have a Adnan and a Malaki!"

"I don't have two personalities. I have a lot of business to take care of on a day-to-day basis, leaving me stressed at times. It doesn't always consist of being around you!"

"Well, is the real you coming out again, Adnan?"

"It's not that I was fake at any time of our relationship. I've always been this way. Lilac, sometimes you are not the easiest person to have a good time with!"

"Well, it does not look like we are going to be lying in the bed, sexing it up tonight. Might as well put back on my pants and sleep in separate rooms, if you like?," said Adnan.

"I never said I wanted to sleep away from you said Lilac. Women, you sure have a way of ruining every moment! You know what, you are giving me too much friction right now. I dont need it said Adnan."

"How many billions does it take to have you, Lilac? You probably have one billion right now, but I have ten!"

"Let me tell you something, homeboy. Remember, Lilac does not need any of them! I do not give a fuck about your billions. I do not give a damn about you, really said Lilac. Sir you cannot imagine how hard it is for me to love someone. Love is hard for me. You are talking to someone that can have the heart of Teflon, steel, and concrete. Do not forget that!"

"Look, Lilac, I don't know what is going on! It seems like we cannot get along nowadays! I would hope to think it's because you are hormonal, if I am not mistaken?"

"Let you tell it, you're a doctor! Or are you? We do live in California where everything is fictitious."

"Fake!"

"Fake information, that is what you are," said Lilac.

"Lilac, there is nothing in the *Webster's Dictionary* that depicts I'm fake! What's fake is me being with you! I've been sending you roses every week!"

"False! You have not been sending me roses. You may be sending them to someone else. You have been sending me lilacs."

"Oh well, excuse me, I was not sending you roses! I was sending you lilacs."

"Not sure who you were sending roses to?"

"There you go again, Lilac! Nitpicking over anything and everything. Can we just get along for tonight? Can we just lie beside each other and enjoy one another before this mood is blown into pieces! Even if we just relax and watch television, that would be a plus."

"You don't want to go eat anymore. What do you want me to do?"

"Are you going to starve the baby?"

"Watch it now, Adnan, before I come pro-choice on your ass in a heartbeat! You do not want me to put on a circus! I have been to plenty of rodeos at my youthful age. This will not be the first!"

"I have too plenty of them! I've been on this earth longer than you!"

"Adnan, this is where you and I split!"

"Depart? Sure, you know I am not going to beg you! I have plenty of roses to send."

"Send your roses to whoever you want to send them to. I no longer need you!"

"Is this a breakup?" said Adnan.

"We need time apart until I have the baby."

"We'll just do that. I can't see any reason why I should remain with a hormonal woman who doesn't want me in her presence. I do not want that type of energy to pass through Lily."

"I peacefully would like us to be apart," said Lilac.

"Lily is my firstborn child! She means the world to me, and you know it, Lilac!"

"Adnan, *if* you really are a doctor—"

"What do you know about my credentials that I do not? All them damn accolades on my wall in my office, and I'm able run an emergency room and have no experience and fake credentials. Let me make this clear, Lilac. I have graduated from medical school with full honors and the top of my class. How dare you insult my intelligence! I went to school in California and studied in Liverpool, to be exact! I traveled the world to learn medicine!"

"You say you have been all over the world to learn medicine, but that's not what your good friend informed me of when this letter was delivered to my house!"

"What friend sent you letter?"

"Frank Gallop! He sent me a letter to let me know that everything about you, especially being a physician, is *fraud*!"

"A fraud! I need to talk to him. There is nothing fraud about me!"

"Your parents paid millions for those credentials hanging in your office. You are running a hospital without medical credentials! Malaki! So who are you talking to? I got you by the *balls*! I really have them in my hands! I can squeeze them whenever I get ready! You have wronged your friend in so many ways until he seeks revenge by sending me this precious letter to let me know that everything you so call accomplished is not real! Adnan, you do not want to get Lilac in the mood to reveal to the world, your secret do you?"

"At this point, Lilac, you are right. This show stops here with you and me. We need to separate!"

"I do not need you around me, Adnan!"

"Lilac, I do not want to be with you or around you! You are beginning to act like your grandmother Jade!"

"Don't you *ever* speak my grandmother's name Jade unless you are saying Jack! Do not ever forget that! They are still powerful even though they are deceased! They live in me, and I know plenty of people, Adnan! Do not ever go there with me! Pill popping-ass self, fake, phony-ass doctor! Without those fake-ass credentials, sir, you are a regular Joe Blow! You need to get yourself moving fast from me and get out of here. Now you know why I question everything about you! I know authentic, and you are a *fake*! Now for the love of me and my unborn child, but guess what, you're not good enough to be my husband! I do not like replicas! I am an original and I thought you were too. But you are as fake as everyone else is in LA! I am going to take my baby with me. now the truth has come out! I can no longer hold in your deception another second! I suggest you hurry and book the next flight to LA!"

"You are right, Lilac. I'm getting ready to get the hell out this hotel room and get far away from you! You are a *black rose*! The *rose* of bullshit!"

"I will be whatever you want me to be, but you better put rich in front of that black rose! Pack your shit and get out of my hotel room!"

"Lilac, you said nothing but a bunch of words that do not connect!"

"Oh, do not forget. Let me show you something else, Adnan."

"What is it now, bitch?"

"These big bags of *pills* that you take several times a day! You are a high-class dope feign dressed up in a tailored silk suit and fine as hell! You are even taking medications to keep your penis up! Make no mistake about it, Adnan, you are taking every pill in the hospital! Simply curious, what type of opiate you have in your home?"

"Lilac, you said enough!"

"You still standing here. You must be high as fuck to stand there and take this verbal ass-whooping I'm handing down to you! Fool!"

"Now like I said, there is a plane that I must catch in the morning to meet with Wafiya! I'm wrapping this relationship up!"

"Thank you, Lilac, for your time and patience. You have a momentous day on purpose, purple-eyed bandit! Glad I did not pack any luggage!"

"Do not forget your pills, Bill!"

CHAPTER 18

Red Dahlia

Now that I got rid of his pill popping ass—he is a nuisance; he should have been more honest with me! Let me call my Hood Bun! This baby does not belong to him, Adnan, anyway!

God knows how long he has been on drugs with his fake ass self! He better hope I do not report his ass to the board of medicine and chair-persons! But I need to find out whether this is his baby or not before I do that. We have a lot of paperwork to sign when it comes to his money! I do not play about my capital. Let me call Loki, 202-584-0000!

"Hello? Hey, Lilac. What is up?"

"What's up, Loki? How are you?"

"Where you at, girl? I'm trying to see you! Let me get some of that warm kitty kat and blow your back out! How my baby doing?"

"We are doing fine, Loki. Why don't you catch a flight up here to New York and chill with Lily and me? I sold a painting today!"

"Lilac, you know am not into all that painting stuff, girl. I'm only into you! I am straight DC, love it so much I had to tat 202 area code!"

"Loki, you make kitty throb when I hear your voice!"

"I will be up there fast to give you some good wood! Can't wait to see you and caress your belly!"

"Before you get on the flight, please stop by Rich Girl Behavior before boarding the plane. I've been following them in a chat group. I admire what they're doing as a formidable group of Black women who are forming ties in order to lift one another up without regard to individual merits, rivalry, or competitiveness, assuaging the myth that Black women are incapable of coexisting peacefully while leveling up! I'm inspired by their tenacity and determination, and I'd like to contribute financially to assist them build their own organization. The organization aims to give back the self-esteem, love, and empowerment that they have received from each other to women who do not—"

"Lilac, what are you doing looking at people on Instagram from DC?"

You'd be surprised at what and who I know, Loki! Obtain their phone number as well so I can deposit money into their account with your help. Do you know about Bird's Kitchen? Yes, she's like family, and since you will be visiting me one day, I might just let you meet Mrs. Bird. Well, Loki, I'm looking forward to that. Bring me some of her famous salmon bites and saucey wings! Her food is allegedly as hot as a torch! "Do not overlook her" is what am hearing! Bring two of each, please!

You're about to screw up and screw Bird's Kitchen and yourself! Her food is good as shit and legendary in DC! Whenever you visit the city, bring your ass right to Benning Road S.E.

"I got you, Lilac, and I will see you on the next flight! I am preparing to catch the flight, Lilac. Send me the ticket information now! You impeded on my plans. Now I have to stop pasts RGB."

A New York Minute

Knock, knock.
"Come on in, Loki!"
"What is up, beautiful!"
"Hi, baby. I missed you!"
"I missed you too. Lilac, I was thinking while on the flight. What do you want from me? We are from two different worlds."

"But that is what I love about you the most. You are different from everyone else around me. You do not have what everybody else has, but I can give it to you."

"I understand you can give me everything, but I am a man. Detailing cars, painting, I'm good with my hands. I can do all kinds of things to make money. Lilac, you cannot buy me. I'm no trick. I am not going to let you take care of me. Let me hold my baby. Your stomach feels so warm."

Loki laid his head on Lilac's lap.

"Now you know I can't take it every time you touch me. My nipples get hard. I am such a horny pregnant woman. Please come and glide your penis where it belongs."

"Girl, you're so good. Like you are so nasty. You like that finger play?"

"I would love for you to do that, but wash your hands first. It feels so good, your finger gliding in and out of my kitty."

"It feels like a blazing inferno inside them walls."

"We only have a couple of hours before I must take my flight. Can you please get undressed?"

"Yes. You know I must recoat before I get in that big-ass bed! Lilac, will you ever stop loving me? Because if you do, you will drive me crazy. I need this. I'm so addicted to you, girl!"

"I know. I am addicted to you, boy! You bring out the young person I have missed. Being with you makes me feel like a kid again."

"I'm glad to make you feel like that. Those people in LA must have really made you grow up fast. Sometimes the things you tell me, Lilac. I'm happy to be where I am."

"Loki, one day, I am going to want you to *man* up and come live with me."

"What! Come on, girl. I am not leaving Washington DC! That is going to be hard for me to do. You are asking a lot of me. I'm a bona fide Washingtonian. One Deuce all the way."

"What you need to be a Californian, with this baby!"

"Lilac, I love you, but I'm not coming to live in LA. I will not be able to afford the things you require to take care of a baby! I'll take care of her with everything I have, from Washington DC."

"Loki, go ahead and take that shower… *Please*!"

"You know what, Lilac? That's what turns me on about you. That accent, your body, and your eyes. You are just so beautiful, darling. I am going to get in the shower."

"You do that."

While he is in there taking a shower, I need to call Anderson and let her know to reschedule the timing because I'm taking a later flight. I need to have what he gives me tonight. I am surely not going back to Adnan. This is what I need to figure out. This cannot be his baby, and I want to take a swab from Loki tonight. DNA time! If this is Adnan's baby, I may be going pro-choice.

But I cannot. I cannot be pro-choice. Lily makes me feel so much more mature, like a woman. I also feel like I have missed so much in my childhood, but anyways…

"Hello."

"Kay Anderson. Hello, darling. How are you? Calling about the ten-o'clock meeting tomorrow?"

"Can we please reschedule the meeting to one o'clock?"

"Let me look at my calendar to see if I have anything available… Yes, I am available. I will go ahead and set up the time and call Theo and Ava and see if I can get them together."

"Okay. We can all meet and discuss where we at with business. Thank you, Kay Anderson."

"Thank you too. Bye," Lilac yelled.

"Oh, I meant to tell you, Loki. I got a call from the front desk. When you brush your teeth, spit in a cup because they are working on the pipes in the infirmary. It's okay to take a bath but don't run the water in the sink."

"Fine time to tell me after I got out of the shower, girl!"

"Spit everything in the cup, please, babe! We don't need that kind of attention, from hotel management."

Fresh and So Clean

"You ready for me, baby?"

"Lilac, man."

"Listen up Thug am going to teach you how to handle me and I got time to do it."

"I am not no damn man! Do not make me come out of my character because you do not know the other side of me! Just because you seen the nice and rich side of me, that does not constitute that I ain't no *beast*! So do not make me flip the script!"

"I did not know you was so rough and tough, Lilac," Loki said with a smile all over his face. "Girl, you dangerous!"

"I am not a soft thug. I'm a hard thug in my own way," said Lilac.

"I'm in love, Lilac, so let me love on you, baby! Because that is what you need! Some of this love I'm about to give you, my baby. The magic potion."

"That is all we need, Loki. I only have a couple of hours before morning."

"Damn, you always in a rush with everything! Glad I have family that exists up here!"

"Come on. Thank you for coming this long way. Now give this baby some loving she has been missing! Let's get this potion to motion!"

"Open them pretty legs and spread them wide from west to east."

"Sound different when you say it the other way around."

"It does. This is normally north to south and east to west," Loki replied.

"Daddy, how much longer do I have to wait?"

"Daddy? So now you've given me my pet name. I am getting ready to put it down on you, girl! Calling me daddy. Get over here!"

Aye am calling the police on that head game Lilac.

That was so damn good and uplifting! Let me hurry up and get dressed. I am so happy Loki came over to get these babies together.

That was some beautiful lovemaking! I am certainly going to do everything possible to get Loki to live with us in Cali, my dear Lily.

I am so glad that Adnan is gone with his crazy ass, but I must deal with him. God knows I do not want to deal with Adnan and Adnani, a whole clown show. He certainly has two personalities, and I cannot deal with them. His whole life is a lie. That's got to be a tough act to follow every day.

He have plenty of nerve running a damn hospital with no real credentials! Boy, I tell you, things that they do in this world, you cannot fathom. You must do your verifications and check everything at least ten times before you figure out who someone really is…especially up in the Hills.

"Hey, Kay. I'm here, I'm getting ready to get dressed now so we can have our family meeting. I must meet up with Adnan later this evening. I hope everything is fine with Daisy, Theo, and Ava."

"Lilac, let me know if Adnan is bothering you. I got your back and will have someone get on his line. There is no air in that. I do not play you know that, right? Because I'm a *bad bitch*," said Atty. Anderson.

"Oh my god, Kay. I never heard you talk like that!"

"I take no Bullshit from no one. That damn Adnan, that is a fast move. After my investigation, I'm going to keep my eye on him. He is not to be trusted, Lilac. At all!"

"Thank you, Kay. You know how much I need you."

"Okay, thank you. I will see everybody by one o'clock."

Let me get dressed. Hope this meeting doesn't go too long. Who they wont see is Sammy-fucked up ass, click up.

"Wafiya, I'm glad to see you. How are you?"

"Fine. How are you?"

"I am doing great."

"Welcome back home."

"Wafiya, I was only gone for overnight."

"Lilac, being away from you is compared to a missing my first everything. Have you been nauseous, sick? Are you hungry? Do you need to eat, said Wafiya."

"I do not have much of an appetite."

"Oh yes, Lilac. I meant to tell you Adnan has been calling here nonstop! What is going on between you two?"

"What is going on is that it is over!"

"Lilac, why would you leave Adnan?"

"Wafiya, there are some things going on that I cannot necessarily tell you. I cannot tell you everything, but I can support you with everything."

"One of those things, huh?" said Wafiya.

"Yes, one of those things. I must meet with the family today with Kay Anderson. I need to contact Daisy to keep her informed of the meeting."

Who's texting me?

> Lilac, I love you.
>
> Lilac: You cannot have me, Adnan! I do not want you! You need to go into a rehab, you are not who you say you are! A person like you will lead me down a twine road to be unsuccessful and miserable. I'm young but am not dumb! I must really look like a fool to you. You wasting my time.
>
> Reply: Lilac, I will never leave you alone. You can bet your bottom dollar on that!
>
> Lilac: We will see about that.
>
> Reply: About what?
>
> Lilac: About leaving me alone! Whatever you are thinking, my advice to you is to stop, Adnan! You will see another side of me you do not even know.
>
> Reply: Please give me another chance. You are carrying my firstborn child!

"Lilac, am calling you back about the swab test," said Atty. Anderson.

"Lilac, it was."

"Who did it come back as being the father?"

"The father certainly is not Adnan."

"Who is this other guy you are dealing with, Lilac?"

"Atty. Anderson, he's not like any of us. He is someone whose finances are not equivalent to any one of us. Do not judge him or me. He does not have a fraction of what we have or who we are, but it is someone that I love. Thank you, Kay, for everything."

CHAPTER 19

Delphinium

"ADNAN. HEY, I NEED TO see you and my baby girl! But I need for us to talk, said Lilac. Things have not been right between us for quite some time. All we do is argue and fuss. We are wasting too much time in my life that I cannot get back, Adnan. Now that I have Lily, I really do not have time for your nonsense. I told you before when the baby was born that you have fifty personalities that I cannot handle. I accepted my reality now. It is time for you to accept yours. I trust that you will say anything and do anything to me! I no longer trust you."

"I know you do not love me anymore, Lilac. I do not take the medication anymore!"

"You think I am supposed to believe what you say just like that? Sir, you manage a hospital with a twisted mind! Anything coming from you, I would never believe a word that comes out of your mouth!"

"I am on my way over there to see my baby!"

"Oh, we are here waiting on you because there is something I need to let you know to your face!"

"Mason! He's on his way over. I'll need you to be on standby."

The Show

"Mason! He is on his way here. I am going to need you to be on standby."

"You know I really do not like Adnan that much! He is always coming in here with an uneasy presence about himself. Jack would never have stood for this if he were here!"

"I know. I am so glad that you are here to help to protect us."

"I am glad I am here to help take care of you, Lilac. I mean, I will do everything I can. Then you just hit this button when you need me because I know he will be here soon."

"Thank you, Mason. Time for the big show. Let me get the baby together. Let me get the family together. Before he comes, there are some things that I need to reveal to him that will guarantee to put an end to this nonsense.

"I am going upstairs to get this paper before he comes. Also, gather up this file… More will be revealed about him to his face!"

"Well, you must have something big for him, huh, Lilac?"

"I do. Whatever it is, it may cause an earthquake."

"Don't do anything that will cause you harm!"

"I won't, Mason."

"Now I will have to pull out my shotgun and blow that motherfucker's head off and go to jail and lie down for the rest of my life. The little bit that I have left, but I will do it for you!"

"Thank you, Mason. I am going to go upstairs now and get dressed. Wafiya is getting Lily prepared for today."

"Lilac, Adnan is here."

"Thank you, Wafiya. I can take it from here."

"Hi, Lilac. Let us just get straight to it."

"How are you, Adnan?"

"I am fine."

"Put her down now," said Lilac.

"This is my baby! I may never have you again, but I certainly got my very own Lily. She has my blood, just as well as she has yours. Do not play with me about my Lily! She may be the same complexion as everyone else in your family, and that is all fine and well. I can admit you guys got dominant genes, but she looks just like me. The same smile, dimples on both sides of her cheeks!"

"Mr. Whacked-Out Adnan, this is not yours, okay? I am going to need you to accept what I am telling you. This is my baby, my baby only! I am the mother, papa!"

"You mix-bred *whore*! You have been saying that before Lily was born! You not playing with a full deck, Lilac!"

"You look like you popped about twenty pills!"

"I probably had popped twenty pills to come and deal with you!"

"We are not going to waste too much time here on any subject but the one I called you here for. As soon as you calm down, I will share it with you."

"Sitting here, thinking of how you never really put full potential into loving me. What was it about me? Was it the flowers that dazzled? Am I too dark for you?"

"Honestly, I really did love you until I found out that you were not who I thought. I don't have time to go back and fix things. I have a whole life ahead of me! I am not wasting any more time with you! I just cannot deal with fake fact findings."

"Put her down! I said this is my baby!," Lilac repeated.

"Here we go again with this BS! Girl, I'm so tired of your crap! You never want me to be close to my Lily. The only real flower that I will ever have, bitch!"

"Listen, Lilac, I kept my ace in the whole, lil girl. I was dating another woman my age. A wealthy, beautiful, established woman, someone I gave up on for you. This is not my only baby, I gave you all my love! I felt sorry for your ass, bitch, when you were lying in the hospital. After you were raped and left for dead, nearly beaten to death! I saw the beauty in you still! The beauty that you thought you would never see yourself! I help you heal with those flowers! I thought that you were something that I can help mold into a better person."

"You are on drugs! How in three hells could you mold me into a better person? I am already a made woman! Let me take you back, sir! The buck stops here! I have been emancipated since I was fifteen years old. I consider myself the sharpest knife in the draw! In fact, the sharpest you have ever had. I do not care who you were seeing!"

"Lilac, you were not ready for me! Now I can admit there were plenty of times I could not be with you because of my family that existed before you!"

"I am glad that you finally admitted that because your friend told me that also in the letter. Wow! You grew a massive set of balls and finally found courage! I was wondering when you were going to confess!"

"That friend can't see the sun with his ass turned up!"

"That is blood on your hands and conscience. I do not want to hear anything about a crime you committed on your own free will. I have nothing to do with that crime that you committed by yourself. You did for nothing!"

"You keep coming at me with these innuendos about nothing! You said nothing but a bunch of words, little girl. Nothing has been mentioned quite a few times in the last minute!"

"It is time for you to know the truth! The fact is, you are a pill-popping ass man and you have a family of three in the Hills with the rest of the pill poppers. A tsunami is coming your way! I suggest you brace yourself for what I am about to expose to you! Remember when you came with me to New York when I sold my last painting, *The Reflection of Reflections*? You, sir, went in the bathroom, called yourself spitting in a cup because you were sick? Whatever you were? I collected your DNA, and I matched it to my baby Lily."

"Give me Lily!"

"You put Lily down. She is not your baby!"

"I am going to kill your ass, prostitute, a whore-ass bitch! You played with my mind one time too many. Now this is it! I want to put my hands around your neck!"

"If you touch me, I will take and beat the hell out of you, *clown*! I will punch you in your face! Get outta here before I call Mason on you and put Lily down!"

"She's not *mine*! Stop playing and joking with me, Lilac!"

"Look at you. Yes, looking like a zombie, still on those drugs. What type of woman do you deal with that would allow you to pop pills and raise a family!"

"I am just like everybody else up here, faking! It is what it is! Nothing is real in the Hills!"

"Something is real, and that is this paper that I am holding in my hand. I need you to have a seat no more bickering and arguing between you and me or me trying to figure out who you are or you trying to figure out who I am. The real thing is, Lily. Not. Belong. To. You. And I need you to accept that before I bring this to your doorstep! I know this is something you would not be ready for, so I am suggesting you pick up your coat, turn around, turn that door-knob, and walk out!"

"Give me that paper!" said Adnan. "You are one of the most hei-nous and wicked women I've put my precious penis in! I have been so helpful to you. I have been everything that you wanted me to be! I cannot believe you have done this to me, Lilac!"

"Do not act like you really care! You cannot care. You have *no* feelings or real emotions. The opiates will not allow it! You spend most of your time snorting coke and popping pills! I stopped want-ing you when I found that out! I am going to put on Lily's clothes, and we are going to get out of here and take a flight to the District of Columbia to see Lily's father, Loki! Adnan, get your stuff and beehive to the door and get in your car. Go home to your family. Enough is enough! Here take this paper with you to keep it for your records."

"So you have been dating somebody else the whole time? It was the friend that sent you the letter?"

"You are so high. How am I going to date the friend that sent the letter when you killed him! Lily's father does not have much, but what he does have are love and reality. He is all mine. He does not have anything to offer but himself! This is my baby, thank you! I will be taking care of my baby by myself. And he would give me the love that I need. One more thing to take with you, Adnan. Self-love is the best love, and no amount of money can buy that! Let me get outta here before things turn ugly! Before I turn you ugly."

"You would never turn me ugly with your Black self, darky!"

"The hell are you calling darky? The mixed breed you are is not even real."

"I am exotic Black!"

"Look at the color of your skin. You are passing for White! I have access to your records. I would have thought all of you were White!"

"Well, that is in my benefit, not yours. Now get out of my house! Lily, stop crying, darling. Momma got you, li'l sugar. Do not complain. Do not cry."

Adnan, go ahead and open the door! What is the plate on the wall, said Adnan.

"What plate?"

"This plate!"

Adnan threw the plate and hit Lilac across the face.

"Aaahhh!" Lilac screamed at the top of her lungs.

"Who's pretty now? Bitch!"

"Mason! Hurry! My face! Adnan picked the designer plate off the wall and threw it at my face! Please, Mason, my face! My baby! Please get my baby!"

"You son of a bitch! I am going to kill you! Wafiya! Get the baby!"

"Help me. Please call 911. My face, my beautiful face!"

"Lilac, lie on the floor," said Wafiya. "I got Lily!"

Mason ran downstairs to get his gun. By then, Adnan had dashed out of the house and ran and jumped into his car and sped off!

"Please get Lily. Please get Lily, baby!"

"Do not worry, baby. Calm down."

"My face. My beautiful face, please. I am never going to be the same again! Please take my precious Lily away!"

To be continued…

ABOUT THE AUTHOR

 LILY WAS BORN TO A beautiful teenager who was fresh off the migration path from rural St. Mary's County, Maryland, to Northeast Washington DC. Accompanied by her parents and eight siblings, the large family was no protection from the city's chaos and trappings. Lily's mother met a handsome but immature young man, "living just enough for the city," addicted to heroin.

Today, Lily enjoys writing, spending time with family, watching movies, and meeting new people. She has been married for a decade (that's a long time!). Lily is a mother to a daughter who has blessed her with her one and only grandchild. She cherishes her sister and step-siblings from near and far. She is incredibly close to her maternal cousins whose mothers were also on that migration for a better life.

Known for telling a good story and making others laugh, Lily always knew that she would craft her own story in book form, but the timing was never right.

One day, Lily had an aha moment. She looked in the mirror and asked herself a question: why are you treated differently by others? She stared at herself so intensely and realized that it was the scar left behind from a traumatic injury, an emotional and physical scar, experienced at nineteen. Lily owned that moment. She decided to reach out to others who had also experienced violations by the hands of another. She would tell a fictional story based on the actual events of that traumatic occurrence, giving birth to *Domestic Lilac*!

CPSIA information can be obtained
at www.ICGtesting.com
Printed in the USA
BVHW040557200223
658834BV00002B/277